Andrew

Andrew had his first Jake Dillon crime thriller published in 2006. He lives in Dorset, where he positions many of Dillon's assignments. Tide Runner is the seventh in the Dillon series. Andrew's writing reflects his interest in travel and his perpetual observation of national security and organised crime. Andrew lives with his family and is currently working on the next gripping novel in the series of Dillon crime thrillers.

Tide Runner

Andrew Towning

Copyright Andrew Towning 2018

All rights reserved. There is no part of this book that may be reproduced or stored in a retrieval system or transmitted in any form, by any means without written permission of Andrew Towning, except by a reviewer who may quote brief passages in their review to be printed or reproduced for social media broadcast.

ISBN-13: 978-1721113392

My thanks to Eloise for her enthusiasm and extensive help with the Dillon process and to Lynn for proofreading and editing of this Jake Dillon Crime Thriller.

Jacket design and photography by
Jack Lodge Photography
www.jacklodgephotography.co.uk

Prologue

The Bahamas

Gulls soared high over New Providence. The light offshore breeze whipped up a salty spray off the crest of each wave as it rolled onto the white sand beach from a sea of brilliant turquoise.

He lounged by the pool of the exclusive Nassau Club hotel, his muscular frame silhouetting the edge of the rattan chair, observing from behind Tom Ford designer sunglasses. A cigarette rested on the edge of the ashtray next to him as he sipped single malt whiskey from an ice-filled tumbler.

The smartphone vibrated next to him. He answered the call, listened and hung up ten seconds later, draping the towel over his shoulder, Dillon left the poolside and walked through exotic gardens to the main reception. He stopped at the concierge's desk, placed the used towel on the counter for a clean one.

The switch was faultless; a plain envelope with a thousand dollars, in exchange for a room key card.

Dillon nodded at the concierge, left and took the stairs up to guestroom thirty-six on the first floor.

Dillon pulled on latex gloves. He made sure no one was in the corridor before letting himself in with the key card. The room felt cool, darkened from the closed shutters. He searched the room, trashing it as he searched through belongings and documents without success, he'd wait for the occupant to return.

Twenty minutes later his patience paid off - the door lock clicked, the door opened, light from the corridor flooded into the semi-darkened room.

* * *

"Hello Brodie!" Dillon stepped into view of the older man. He held a Beretta in his left hand levelled at the stomach of the former head of Ferran & Cardini's special projects section.

Brodie Stevens stood motionless, a blank expression across

his face; a pro to the end. He recovered his composure and stepped into the room and slumped into one of the easy chairs.

"I was wondering when you'd appear, Jake."

"Is that so, Brodie? Well I haven't come here to discuss the weather. You know why I'm here and you know who sent me."

"I imagine the partners want me back." The words held no emotion.

"You embarrassed them and you tried to set me up for a fall. Fooling every one of us into thinking you were in fear of your life. The excessive drinking, hiding yourself away in your flat, it was subterfuge, carried out to throw me off the scent."

"Yes, sorry but I couldn't risk you getting too close, you see."

Dillon watched the older man for a moment. "Where is the African black diamond?"

"What makes you think I've got it?"

"We recovered The Spirit of Grisogono along with an assortment of other stuff that was held by the Black Panther crime syndicate. But the African black diamond is still missing, I then got to thinking..."

"And what, has this got to do with me?"

Dillon raised the Beretta and screwed on the silencer. He looked at the older man as he was doing it.

"This gun, if you're wondering, was used in a murder committed during a mugging on the island a week ago. What's that got to do with you you're asking yourself. I've turned this room over to make it appear as it was a robbery. If I shot you, the authorities might look for a burglar and you'd become just another statistic.

So, here's the rub Brodie. My flight back to London leaves in just under three hours. I'll give you one chance to tell me what I want to know. And then, I'm going to cause you immense pain. The first bullet will be in the shoulder. It won't kill you but it will be extremely painful and from this range it might even go out the other side. You've got ten seconds!" Dillon glanced at his Omega.

There was a tense silence in the room. Then the gun spat, the bullet hitting its mark - the older man thrown onto the polished stone floor.

Brodie pressed his hand against the bullet wound to stem

the bleeding. "You bastard - you didn't have to do that," the words came angrily from between clenched teeth. The former spy glowered at Dillon as he pulled himself back onto the chair. "Tell me Brodie or, I will shoot you in the other shoulder." The older man pointed at a large red suitcase standing in the corner of the room. Dillon backed up to the case and looked at it.

"Turn the case over and grab hold of the left hand front wheel."

Dillon turned the case over to expose the base and the wheels. "What now?"

Brodie Stevens instructed Dillon. "Turn the spindle two times clockwise and four times anti-clockwise and then pull it sharply."

Dillon carried out the instruction and the wheel came away in his hand.

"Now twist the two halves of the sphere and they'll come apart."

Dillon extracted the black diamond from its lead-lined hiding place and held it up to the light.

"I'll give you top marks for cunning Brodie. Packing the diamond inside the wheel -pure genius." Dillon placed the diamond in his pocket.

"Okay, you've got what you came to retrieve. What now?"

Dillon looked at the older man without pity. All he felt was repugnance for his deviousness.

The trigger responded to his touch. Bridie remained sitting upright in the easy chair, eyes open, a narrow trickle of blood running from the tiny hole in his forehead.

It seemed apt that he met his end in this way.

Dillon tossed the Beretta out through the open window into the shrubbery; pulled off the latex gloves he'd been wearing since arriving and didn't glance back as he walked out of the room.

Dillon made his way back to the poolside. He lit a cigarette, sipped at his drink and sent an encrypted message to the partners of Ferran & Cardini.

Problem erased - The African star is safe.

Chapter 1

One Mile
The coast of the British
Channel Island of Guernsey
February

Dan Lacroix sometimes questioned why he'd got himself involved in such a dreadful business, overwhelmed with the direction his life was taking and where it would end.

No matter how many layers of clothing Dan Lacroix put on, the chill inside the cabin penetrated right through to his core. Outside the night was pitch dark and artic; the Tide Runner was entering hazardous waters.

He knew from past visits that lethal rocks were hiding just below the surface of the black water. He guessed where they were as the boat ran without navigational aids, which wasn't helping but essential to cloak them from the coastguard.

A strong wind blew from the south-west across the northern coast of France, driving the waves into whitecaps, scattering salt spray against the windscreen of the shabby fifty-six-foot boat. Dan Lacroix eased back on the throttles and adjusted his course, straining his eyes into the darkness, waiting for the signal to come from the shore.

He pulled out a small hipflask from the inside pocket of his parka, aware of a trembling in his fingers. He was tired and scared but he kept himself alert and the money he received from this trip was too good to miss. Cash up-front and tax-free, which was more than he could earn from an entire season of fishing trips. He'd no option but to work for Liam Finnegan.

His seven-year-old daughter suffered from a rare genetic condition, doctors telling him her eighth birthday would be her last unless he could raise two hundred thousand Euros for lifesaving treatment in Switzerland.

The light flashed and after a moment it appeared again before vanishing. Fora moment he wondered whether he had imagined it. Running a hand over his eyes he squinted, watching through the night-vision scope, until the dot of light appeared again. Then he pulled himself together and used a two-way radio to alert the Irishman.

There were heavy footsteps on the companionway, Liam Finnegan emerged. He had been drinking again and the smell of rum and cigarettes sour on the clean salt air, made Lacroix nauseous. Liam Finnegan shunted him aside and took the wheel.

Finnigan drew on his cigarette, spotting the signal on shore, just off to the port-side. He nodded to himself, increased the speed and altered course. The boat rushed into the darkness. He took a small bottle of rum from his pocket, emptied the contents and tossed it through the open door and over the side rail.

In the dim light of the cabin he appeared wraithlike, a macabre image with mousey brown hair that clung to his skull. His face was skeletal with the eyes of a hog and a bulbous nose covered in leathery skin coarsened by years of salt air, boozing and poor diet.

Dan Lacroix trembled at the very sight of the Irishman. Finnegan smirked, Lacroix knew what the Irishman was thinking, it always involved being mocked.

Finnegan grabbed Lacroix by the shirt collar, one hand still on the wheel and pulled him close. The Irishman's rancid breath and filthy stale smelling clothes filled his nostrils. Lacroix strained to get away.

"Stay scared, that's right. Get outside and make the dinghy ready."

With a shove, he propelled into the black of night; Lacroix grabbed hold of the side rail to save himself from going over the side. He looked at the Irishman, pure rage running through him, tempered only by his own meekness. He felt his way along the side rail towards the stern of the boat and dropped to one knee beside the Mercury Quicksilver dinghy. Drawing out a nine-inch stiletto switchblade knife from his pocket he held the line he'd tied the dinghy with and cut through it. The slender razor-sharp blade mesmerised him, he thought of Finnegan with his throat cut open from a single draw of the blade.

The thought of this act made his stomach churn, bile rising into his mouth. He closed the knife, getting to his feet and took a deep lungful of salt air and waited at the stern rail.

The fifty-six-foot boat rushed into the darkness, the flashlight signalled from the beach again. As Finnegan cut the power the bow dropped, slowed and the current took hold of the Tide Runner. The beach was a hundred yards away marked by the whitecaps crashing on to the shore. Lacroix released the electric anchor winch as Finnegan moved to the stern and heaved the dinghy over the side on his own and pulled it back in by the line. Lacroix jumped into the small craft.

"Get back here as quick as you can, hear me. I want out of here as soon as possible or we'll miss the tide."

Water slopped in the bottom of the dinghy, unwelcome, as Lacroix took hold of the outboard motor and dropped it into the water. He pulled the starter cord and the single propeller came to life. That anxious feeling rising again as was the case these days. This beach was unknown terrain in spite of the fact he had been there at least a dozen times before, for the same reason.

As he approached the secluded cove he always had the same nagging feeling; what if this was the last time? The police could be waiting. He might end up in a prison cell.

Raised high on a rolling wave as it came closer to the shore, then plunging across the line of foaming spray onto the sand. Lacroix lifted the dinghy's outboard motor out of the water, locking it in place, slipped over the side and pulled the dinghy up the beach a short distance.

He swung the bow round so the small craft was facing back out to sea once again, crouched out of the wind and rain, waiting just out of sight. After five minutes an intense light pierced the darkness, blinding him.

He stood up and held his hand to the light. A calm public-school accent came out of the darkness.

"You're late. Let's get on with this."

It was the Englishman again: Elliott Stark. Lacroix could tell, even in the pitch dark, by the clipped accent and arrogant manner. He was the only man he had known Finnegan show any respect. He was a shadowy figure as was the man with him. They spoke together in Swedish, a language Lacroix had no grasp but recognised; the other man stepped forward and got into the dinghy, squatting on the bench in the prow. Lacroix pulled the dinghy off the sand, the draw of the waves making it arduous to board. Stark pushed the dinghy to deeper water and scrambled over the side.

Finnegan was waiting at the stern rail of the Tide Runner when they reached the boat, his cigarette glowing in the darkness. The passenger ascended the ladder first and Stark followed with his overnight bag. By the time Lacroix had pulled himself on deck, Stark and the passenger were in the cabin.

Finnegan helped him get the dinghy over the rail and left Lacroix to secure it to the deck as he moved back to the bridge. A moment later the powerful diesel engines came to life as they moved out to sea. Lacroix secured the dinghy to the deck, checked around, made tidy and then stood for moment dreading having to go back inside the cabin.

Stark was standing on the bridge alongside Finnegan drinking whisky from the bottle, the Englishman's chiselled pleasing face contrasting with Finnegan, champagne and ale. One was a common street brawler, the other a well-bred and cultivated toff. And yet, they got on well with each other, something Lacroix could never work out why.

Lacroix entered the bridge and the two men stopped talking, looking at him as if he were an intruder. Lacroix shuddered and made his way to the day cabin.

* * *

They were making good time with the weather being generous to them as they crossed the English Channel but as dawn came so did the fog. Lacroix was at the wheel and the screen on the console told him they were four miles off the Dorset coast. He spoke into the two-way radio and a while later Finnegan appeared. He looked dreadful from lack of sleep and too much whisky, his eyes were bloodshot and his skin had the texture and pallor of death. "What is it?"

Lacroix nodded at the weather. "It's not good, there's fog with us to the coast."

"How far off the coast?"

"We're out four miles according to the radar," Lacroix studied the radar screen.

Finnigan pushed past the first mate and shoved him out of

the way. Stark appeared at the top of the companionway.

"What's the problem?"

Finnegan glanced back. "Nothing I can't handle."

Stark walked out on deck, steadying himself against the rail. The boat pitched and rolled on the swell, his face impassive, calm and yet a small muscle just under his right eye twitched involuntary. He turned and brushing past Lacroix moved back into the warmth of the boats interior.

Lacroix pulled up the hood on his parka, thrust his hands into his pockets and stood by the port-side rail. In the grey light of dawn, the boat looked grubbier and sea-worn and made to look sea-battered and slow. A vessel that looked as if it had been through tough times and infrequent servicing. Moisture beaded everything, grey tendrils caressing Lacroix's face with the touch of the dead. He breathed in the early morning salt air laden with the familiar smell of seaweed.

Unease was knotting his stomach causing painful cramps, dew-drops hanging on the end of his nose. He was a nervous wreck struggling to get a cigarette out of the packet with numb fingers.

The boat slipped through the water towards the Dorset coast cloaked by the dense fog. Lacroix took one last drag from the cigarette and flicked the butt over the rail. As he turned to go back inside he saw the sleek black shape cutting across the bow of the Tide Runner, one hundred feet away.

Finnegan had seen the silhouette of the slender craft and was reducing speed as Stark appeared on deck. He moved to the rail and stood there looking through binoculars at the circling power craft. The radio inside the bridge sounded, the warning given. Stark turned and looked at Finnegan, his face ashen in the early morning light.

"They're ordering us to stop engines. They want to board us."

"What the hell?" Stark looked panicky. "Damn, it's a fast response coastguard unit in one of the latest military supplied power craft. They use them for patrolling this part of Channel and come out from Poole Harbour. We need to lose them in the fog." Stark looked at Finnegan.

Lacroix's dread rising from the pit of his stomach.

"The boat they're using will go well over sixty knots and

is armed, Mr Stark. We don't stand a hope in hell against it."

Stark grabbed him by the throat, squeezing with his forefinger and thumb either side of his wind pipe.

"Five to ten years in a prison cell, that's what you'll get if they board this boat and find our friend. Now get out of my way and keep your mouth shut."

He nodded to Finnegan, dashed across the cabin and descended below. The twin Volvo Penta inboard engines burst into life as Finnegan opened the throttles. Finnegan spun the wheel at the same time and the Tide Runner responded by heeling over for a moment before surging forward into the cover of the dense fog.

They became invisible - hidden from sight. Engines stopped, electronic devices switched off. Silence, no one spoke, there were footsteps coming up the companionway, Stark appeared with the passenger. He was a man in his mid-fifties, of average height, well-groomed and wearing a long camel overcoat with the collar up around his neck. He looked around confused by the commotion. His tone quiet and calm. Stark spoke to him in Swedish. The man nodded and moved as ordered. Stark moved with him towards the stern rail, pulling a thin wire out of the base of his wristwatch. It happened in an instant that if you blinked, you'd have missed what happened next. The garrotte extended around the man's throat cutting into his windpipe before he could call out, dropping him without a sound or any fuss to the deck. Stark removed the wire, wiped the blood from it and retracted it back into the base of the wristwatch.

The Englishman moved with speed and nimbleness as he unfastened the stern rail and rolled the body overboard. In the thick fog this act of callous murder was unnoticed; the English Channel embraced the dead man's body.

Finnegan glanced at his wristwatch; enough time had passed since the coastguard had demanded to board the them, so he had powered up the inboard diesels and the fifty-six-foot craft surged forward. Lacroix couldn't believe what he had just seen. Something out of a nightmare...

Stark turned and walked back towards where Lacroix was standing and struck him in the face, sending him sprawling to the deck. "Now get up and do what you're paid for. Look as if you're working on fishing lines, or you'll get the same as him."

Stark strode back into the cabin. Lacroix lay there for a moment, then got to his feet and stumbled along the deck. There was blood where the man had bled out.

The deck rolled over to the starboard side as Finnegan spun the wheel again. Lacroix lost his balance. He fell forward on to the blood-soaked deck, smeared his hands in the gore, puke rose into his mouth.

The Tide Runner remained shrouded by the fog and out of sight of the coastguard as they circled round for a while longer before making the run back into Poole. At the wheel Finnegan had opened another bottle of rum and was swigging from it. As Stark passed him he laughed.

"We've lost the coastguard but had better keep a sharp eye out on our approach into Poole."

"Your luck is with us Mr Stark. Although, it's a pity the consignment makes this trip an expensive one!" The Irishman's resentment quite evident.

"That's life, Finnegan." Stark was unconcerned and nodded to where Lacroix was crouching by the stern rail, staring out into the fog.

"Can we trust your first mate?"

"He'll do as he's told. He knows I'll rip off his head if he ever speaks a word of what happens on this boat. Or, he might have to go for a swim." Finnegan laughed.

"What will you tell them back at the boatyard?"

Stark shook his head. "Leave it."

He went along the deck and stood, a hipflask of whisky in his hand.

"You'd better have a drink."

Lacroix raised his head. His eyes full of despair. "Was it necessary to kill him, Mr Stark?"

Stark's flaxen hair glinted in the early morning sun, making him look much younger than his fifty-six years. He stared at Lacroix, his face showing a deep concern. Sighing, he crouched and produced an Uzi 9mm pistol from under his jacket.

Stark stroked the blue metal casing without even a trace of mockery, then released the safety catch.

"Your kid, Lacroix," his voice was gentle, his face keeping its composure for a moment.

"Mr Stark?" Lacroix's heart felt as if it had stopped

beating for a moment.

"One word of what occurred on board this boat today and I will put a bullet in her head. You understand me?"

Lacroix turned away, stomach heaving with nausea again. Stark stood up and walked along the deck and stood at the entrance to the cabin.

"What happened? Is Lacroix okay?" Finnegan demanded.

"Lacroix understands." Stark took a deep lungful of salt air and smirked.

"It's a fine morning to be at sea, Mr Finnegan."

Chapter 2

London
April

Heavy rain deluged the streets of the city, the weather that reduces one of the world's great metropolises to desolation.

Dillon abandoned the black London cab at Horse Guards Avenue and walked toward the Houses of Parliament. He turned up the collar of his black trench-coat as he passed through the Victoria Embankment gardens. There was only one thing he liked better than rain and that was heavy rain, the kind that made people scurry frenetically for cover. An eccentricity from his youth, he supposed, or was there a more complex explanation? Rain placed one in an insular private world, which could be useful.

He paused under the shelter of a tree to light a cigarette, a tall ruggedly handsome man with classically good looks taken from his Irish father and English mother. Dillon continued on towards the Ministry of Defence. He studied those around him as he walked. A man sitting on a park bench speaking on his mobile phone who glanced up from under his umbrella as Dillon passed. A mother, pushing a querulous screaming child in a covered buggy, looking frazzled. Men, their faces told the story, as they trudged to their day of nine-to-five boredom. A smile crossed his face as he walked past them.

Steps down leading to a maintenance access hatch were revealed at low tide. The Thames slapped against the concrete. Dillon stood at the top of the embankment for a moment, glanced both ways before descending to a concrete walk way. The electronic key he held unlocked the solid metal door with a single click of the button, releasing the airtight seal, the door swung inwards. He stooped to enter the maintenance tunnel.

He walked for two hundred feet to the other end, got in the elevator and a moment later got out far below ground. They were expecting him and a uniformed police officer escorted him along a series of other corridors, each one stretched into infinity.

He was led through a heavy-looking metal door into a high-tech operation centre where Dunstan Havelock greeted him.

"Jake, welcome to my new office."

"It's different I'll give you that Dunstan."

"The Home Secretary moved here along with a few members of staff."

"Where is - here?"

"We are one hundred feet below the Ministry of Defence. This tunnel network doesn't appear on any blueprint of the building or for this part of London, a legacy from the Cold-War and the nuclear threat." The Home Secretary's senior advisor walked across to his desk and sitting, asked,

"Jake, please forgive me, I'm being rude. Would you like a coffee?"

"A coffee, thank you Dunstan." Dillon sat on the swivel chair opposite him.

"You're wondering why I asked you to come here today?"

"The thought had occurred to me, Dunstan." Dillon replied sarcastically. "It obviously wasn't out of friendship because you would have asked me to your house for dinner. So, it must be a problem the Home Secretary has."

Dillon's gaze wandered around the low-ceilinged room. A large plasma screen filled most of the end wall and two smaller screens linked to computers had technicians monitoring them.

Dunstan Havelock walked over and spoke to the technicians. The large plasma screen on the wall came to life with the object of his visit laid out on an autopsy table covered with a green surgical sheet.

The coroner stared down at the corpse. looked up at the camera lens and spoke quietly into the microphone. "Good morning gentlemen. I'll start by saying the body is bloated and devoid of pigmentation from prolonged submersion in salt water."

"Let us see it, professor. We're not squeamish." Dunstan instructed.

The professor had a technician pull back the sheet.

Dillon moved closer to the screen. He'd seen death many times in its many guises but this was something new. He stared, a slight frown on his face.

"How long was he in the water?"

"I estimate six weeks give or take a day or two. The fish of course have been at the corpse but otherwise we've got enough of him."

"Can you be certain of the timescale?"

"We did tests to pinpoint this."

"So?" Dunstan Havelock asked bluntly.

"So - even though the submersion in salt water plays havoc with the skin cells and internal organs, the body can give us a timeline. I'd say this one came from the north, say Scandinavia."

"He does have that look about him." Dillon commented. Adding, "What was the original cause of death?"

"It was caused by a garrotte, cut clean through his windpipe."

"Thank you, professor, is there anything else?"

The professor held up an evidence bag to the camera. "We dug this out of the man's neck, just below his right ear."

"Can't see - what is it?" Havelock demanded.

"An RFID chip by the looks of it." Dillon said.

"You're absolutely right, Mr Dillon - a Radio Frequency Identification chip to give its full title."

"Please have that bag and its contents over to my office within the hour, marked for my eyes only. The Home Secretary has authorised that the body be disposed of, cremation only. Use the usual firm and have the paperwork sent to my office." The frown lines on Havelock's forehead were furrowed like a ploughed field. He turned and asked both technicians to leave.

"Okay, so it's ashes to ashes for that boy but who was he and why the urgency to dispose of the body?" Dillon said, sipping his coffee.

"That man Jake was a member of an extremist terrorist organisation calling themselves, Red November. That's it for now."

"Unusual, isn't it?"

"That's an understatement. The Home Secretary wants answers Jake. He wants them fast."

"Then why aren't you using your own people. They're more than capable?"

"Too many leaks within the service - we can't afford this to get into the public domain, that's why! We definitely can't afford the press getting wind of this."

"To whom will I be reporting?"

"You will report directly to the Home Secretary through me."

"So, why are we waiting? You'd better brief me about the assignment."

"Sir Hector Blackwood, head of covert operations will complete your briefing".

* * *

The pathologist's assistant had been in the lab all the time the professor had been video linked to Havelock and Dillon. Lighting a cigarette, he leaned against the wall outside the mortuary and wondered about Dillon. There was something askew with him. He was obviously English with Mediterranean thrown in giving his skin a certain swarthiness, but something wasn't quite right. His eyes were cold and expressionless, seemed to look right through you and said nothing about the person but instead warned of what might lurk under the surface.

The assistant shuddered and untied the bag of clothes that the dead man had arrived in, such as it was. He rifled through each pocket in turn in case anything had been missed during the search. He took a pair of scissors and cut out each pocket lining to search for anything that might have been concealed there.

The silver coloured vial had been woven into the fabric so well that he had almost missed it. It looked like it might be valuable. He held it between his forefinger and thumb as he held it up to the light. What was it? He would take it to a friend who might be able to tell him. In the meantime, he had a body to cremate. He took an evidence bag and placed the object inside, putting it in the zipped compartment of his wallet.

Pushing the trolley through to the crematorium next door he rolled the body into the oven. Closed the inner glass door and pushed the start button and waited for the flames to appear, initially as a flicker and then engulfing the distended body. The outer metal door closed and the cremation was under way, this would take around two to three hours.

He stepped outside, stood under the entrance canopy and lit another cigarette. It was still raining heavily, water overflowed from the gutters but he was okay leaning up against the wall. He pulled out the clear evidence bag from his wallet and held it up to the light. What was this tiny tube hiding?

* * *

It was almost six months since Dillon had visited the house overlooking Kensington gardens and returning was like returning home after a long absence. Not so strange, perhaps, when one considered the life he had led for the last ten years as a field officer with Ferran & Cardini International. That little-known section of the British intelligence service had handled the business no other agency wanted or knew what to do about. The organisation disbanded on the order of the Prime Minister in 2016 after the Brodie Stevens affair raised security issues and major organisational failings.

He strode up to the top of the steps and pressed the bell beside the polished stainless-steel plate that carried the name International Media agency. The door was opened by a stocky muscular man somewhere in his late-fifties wearing a black suit who positively beamed a welcome.

"Good to have you back, Mr Dillon. You're looking very well, sir - if you don't mind me saying, sir."

"It's good to be back, Duff."

"Sir Hector is expecting you, sir. Please go straight up to the conference room, sir. I'm assuming you haven't forgotten the way, sir?"

"I'm pleased you still have that dry sense of humour, Duff. I think I can find my own way, thank you."

Dillon walked through the palatial hall to the wide staircase, mounting two steps at a time he quickly got up to the second floor. Nothing had changed. Not a thing. It was just like it had been when he had left ten years earlier to join Ferran & Cardini International.

When he entered the anteroom, Phoebe Young was seated at her desk. She glanced up and removed her designer specs with a smile that was warm and friendly.

"Good morning Mr Dillon, Sir Hector is waiting."

"Thank you, Miss…"

"Phoebe Young, sir."

"Thank you, Phoebe. You can dispense with the sir. It's Jake, or if you prefer, my friends call me Dillon."

"I'll remember. Now, have you had time to read the email I sent earlier?"

"Not really. I glanced at it briefly but haven't had time to study it as I had to talk to the professor about the body pulled out of the sea."

"It really would have been a good idea to at least know the key points of the situation before seeing Sir Hector." She pressed the intercom. "Jake Dillon is here, Sir Hector."

"Okay."

"Please go through, Sir Hector will see you now."

"He hasn't changed, then."

Dillon knocked once on the highly polished mahogany double doors. He didn't wait for an acknowledgement and as he walked into the conference suite, a tiny flicker of excitement moved coldly in his psyche.

* * *

Sir Hector Blackwood hadn't changed in the slightest. The same dark blue pinstriped suit, crisp white shirt from the same distinguished tailor. The same Old Etonian tie with a precise Windsor knot tied and not a thinning hair out of place. But most of all there was the same stare, cold, from behind horn rim specs. He couldn't even manage a smile.

"Good morning, Dillon. It's good to see you here on time," he said, as if he didn't mean a single word of it. "Please sit."

"I'll get straight to the point. I don't like your methods and I don't want you working for this department. Unfortunately, I have no say in the matter on this occasion and as you have the full weight of the Home Secretary behind you I have to accept the situation."

"Thank you, Sir Hector. It's what I like most about you - your honesty, sir."

"Still belligerent I see."

"I try my best when the occasion calls, Sir Hector." Dillon retorted drily.

Sir Hector ignored the comment getting straight down to business. "The medical officer informs me that she has passed you physically fit for active service it would seem. Although you did not attend the psychiatric evaluation. Any particular reason?"

"It clashed with an appointment with my tailor, Sir Hector".

"Damn it all, Dillon. It's this maverick attitude of yours that I dislike the most."

"We don't have to like each other Sir Hector. You do your job and I'll do mine."

"You've seen the body that was pulled out of the Channel?"

Dillon nodded, "Who is he?"

Sir Hector tapped the touch screen set in to the glass table top and a file appeared.

"He was born and lived in Sweden. His name was Alek Bergfalk."

"Bergfalk - meaning mountain falcon," Dillon interjected.

"That may be so but he's also known to Interpol by aliases and that's not one of them. We couldn't find out who he was from his fingerprints as the fish had done a proper job on them. His dental records on the other hand, were most helpful along with the RFID chip the professor dug out of his neck. This told us exactly who he was."

Dillon shrugged. "Was the RFID chip encrypted?"

"Yes, the encryption was a challenge for the technicians, to say the least. Luckily, the team had seen this level of security once before and was able get in eventually and extract the information."

"Two years ago, an American politician was assassinated in Paris; it was the Red November group who claimed responsibility."

"Your point is?"

"At the time, there was a massive manhunt by the CIA, Interpol and MI6 but not one of them could find the shooter. Until, two months ago when GCHQ intercepted an encrypted email that mentioned an assassination planned for a high-profile British political figure. The name of the assassin was to be code named - mountain falcon."

"That's interesting but it could simply be a coincidence. Now, can we get on with this?"

"Of course - as you say it might just be a coincidence. But somebody cut this man's throat in a very professional manner and then dumped his body into the sea. Whoever killed him was in a tremendous hurry. Otherwise, he would have been weighted down and the body would have gone straight to the bottom and vanished. Instead it was carried by the tidal movements for four or five weeks until it was washed up on a beach. So why was he killed?"

"In the first place, it didn't happen in quite that way. He was brought ashore by the Coastguard out of Fareham in Hampshire; a yachtsman spotted something floating in the water, took a closer look and saw that it was a partially clothed body."

Sir Hector tapped the screen, an image appeared. "This image was taken of Alek Bergfalk in 2016. You will note that he is wearing army fatigues as are the other men with him and at first glance looks like a group of soldiers enjoying a drink together."

"Where was the photo taken?"

"The Ukraine but it's not the location that's of interest, rather it's the group of soldiers that's caused a bit of a stir in certain quarters. The men standing with Bergfalk are all known mercenaries and extremist sympathisers who go wherever the war takes them."

"Bergfalk must have had an enormous amount of pull to get these men to come together all at once. It does present the question of why they are meeting in what looks like a military facility in that particular territory." Dillon interjected.

Sir Hector leaned back in his seat. "Let me tell you a short story Dillon. On the 28th February 1998, the conflict in Kosovo broke out. Alek Bergfalk arrived in the former Yugoslavia when he was twenty-one and joined the KLA, Kosovo Liberation Army at the start of the crisis..."

"Where was he stationed?" Dillon interrupted.

"After a week of basic training he was sent straight to the front line and saw action from the moment he got there. A month later his commander had him transferred to a unit primarily involved with weapons smuggling from Albania.

We think that the chip was implanted to keep track of him. Within nine months he had returned to Sweden where he associated himself with anyone who could be used to make money for himself and the cause in Kosovo. When the conflict came to an end, he joined the Red November group and made it his business to find out and master all aspects of their organisation inside and out."

"What did he do next?"

"Take your pick. He pulled together his mercenary buddies and formed an organised crime syndicate involving themselves in wholesale prostitution, drug smuggling, illegal weapons trading and people smuggling to name but a few. When that wasn't enough they moved into major league stuff a year later, including armed robberies of banks and internet scams."

"Wasn't he a lovely man? So, what was the catalyst for his murder?" Dillon asked, leaning back on his chair.

Sir Hector shook his head. "He was on his way to the UK aboard a boat that is privately owned, which means he didn't want anyone to know his whereabouts. We checked with the Coastguard. They informed us that one of their patrols working out of Poole in Dorset attempted to board a fifty-six-foot craft flying UK insignia. They ignored the order taking evasive action and losing them in thick fog.

The skipper closed down the boats navigational, electrical and mechanical systems. The Coastguard reported they remained in the area for a while before they were called to another interception. The report states one thing that is probably the most important piece of information. The boat must have been fitted with a signal jamming device on-board and this skipper knew exactly what he was doing."

"Was Bergfalk married?"

"No. He lived on his own but always had a beautiful woman on his arm and never the same one!" Sir Hector raised his right eyebrow.

"What about brothers or sisters?"

"There's a sister, Agneta. She lives here in London and has been under surveillance by MI5 for about six months. This has been intensified since her brother's body was washed up on our shores." Sir Hector brought up the image on the large screen.

"Is this Agneta?" Dillon asked, studying the image - the

piercing blue eyes, smooth porcelain like complexion, elfin cut golden hair and slender neck. She was very beautiful.

"Yes. She's younger than Alek Bergfalk by eight years, making her forty-seven. She was privately educated in Sweden then attended Oxford where she studied law, graduating with a Bachelor of Law degree. She then flew through her Bar exams and was head hunted by the best chambers in London's Inns of Court.

Agneta Bergfalk is no time waster and quickly climbed up through the ranks. Her success in court as defence council is impeccable and impressive."

"She's intelligent and beautiful, a dangerous combination!" Dillon remarked.

"Nothing reported by the surveillance team, although the tech boys have found anomalies in her personal life over the past ten years."

"Inconsistencies - her life must be fairly irregular I would have thought."

"Quite so, these are irregularities of a financial nature. Agneta Bergfalk has had regular sums deposited from an untraceable source, into an account held by her in Guernsey."

"How much are we talking?"

"Each payment is never less than a quarter of a million pounds. Sterling! Interpol has tried to trace the source. It's a numbered account and in a territory, that has a policy of non-disclosure. So far Agneta has had over ten million pounds paid to her from the same source. Two months ago, she paid out half a million pounds to a numbered account in Switzerland."

"Do you know who the recipient is?"

"Too soon to say but we're working on the Swiss bankers."

"Was Alek Bergfalk under surveillance?"

"Yes, Interpol and MI5 had them both under surveillance for about six months. Interpol followed him all over Europe, tracking him to Florence where he had two meetings with unknown males during the evening he arrived. The next morning, he boarded a train to Rome, where he checked into the Hassler hotel and took the 6th floor Presidential suite San Pietro. Bergfalk didn't leave his suite during the forty-eight hours he was there and he had no guests either."

"You mean the surveillance team didn't spot anyone! They obviously missed someone."

"I can't say one way or another, Dillon. But it's a possibility given that the Hassler is one of the busiest hotels in Rome. Apparently, Interpol had people all over that hotel and a photographic team located in a nearby building with a clear view of the main entrance…"

"His visit to Rome is still a mystery and for nearly six weeks his whereabouts were unknown. Then he reappeared washed up, half naked with his throat garrotted, on an English beach" Dillon interjected.

"Quite. It's obvious that he was attempting to enter the UK unseen but for what reason?" Sir Hector paused for a moment "If he had been found on board that boat it would have meant a stay in a prison cell for certain for him and anyone caught with him."

Dillon thought of the recent terrorist atrocities in Paris and Berlin. "Someone put him over the side into the Channel but the question is, who?"

"There are criminals making vast sums of money transporting illegals. Anyone who can't get a visa through the conventional channels can find someone who will take their money. Most of them at the hands of amateurs. It's the professionals who're getting away with it, the people with the organisation. There's a pipeline running all the way up from the most southerly tip of Italy. The Italian police have been informed as have the French authorities. They've both been running checks on the known organised traffickers but have come up with nothing we didn't already know."

"That's disappointing."

"What is interesting, is the information we got back from the Channel Islands. Amongst others there's a boat called the Tide Runner that makes regular fishing runs to Jersey and Guernsey, sailing out of Poole harbour."

Dillon tapped the screen and the image file opened and scrolled through the images it contained. There was several of Alek Bergfalk over a four-year period, in military uniform and others of him dressed in smart business-like suits. There was only one family image of Bergfalk with an arm around the shoulders of his sister Agneta. Dillon continued to scroll through the other files and then glanced at Sir Hector.

"With due respect, Sir Hector. This is work for the police or the border agencies. This department wouldn't usually get involved."

"The UK border agency and the Coastguard both advised that the file should be passed onto the anti-terrorism squad. They then submitted the file to the Home Secretary's office and Dunston Havelock decided that the file should be passed to MI5. I took one look at it and agreed with Havelock that this investigation called for the talent you have, Dillon."

"The last time I worked for this department, it involved me spending three months chasing an organised crime syndicate half way across the UK. I was driven off the road and then held by two very large Russians while their boss used me as a punch bag and I almost lost my life," Dillon said. "What is it you want from me?"

"Let me answer that by asking you this. Are you fit enough, both in body and mind, for field work?" Sir Hector held Dillon's gaze.

"As you are fully aware Sir Hector, I've been training with the regiment in Hereford for the two last months."

Sir Hector tapped the screen and Dillon's personnel records appeared.

"Remarkably, you passed every test they threw at you with ease." Sir Hector looked up under bushy eyebrows. "One thing caused concern during your sessions with the doctors, Dillon."

"Oh, what might that be?"

"When they tested you with psychometric methods, you passed with a near perfect score. Unusual! The other element of your training that raised an eyebrow or two was the virtual reality simulation to rescue injured personnel from a hostile held village. You were monitored throughout the thirty-minute mission during which time your heartbeat hardly altered."

"I don't faze easily."

"Well, their report suggests that you're suppressing something deep in your psyche. So, I'm asking you Dillon, should I be worried?"

"No, Sir Hector nothing to worry about," Dillon said smiling.

Dillon knew exactly what it was the shrinks were referring

to. And yet again, he had managed to hide the Dillon who loitered in his subconscious and came out to play when life and limb were threatened. The dark side of his psyche heightened every sense in his body. Turned a world of chaos into a world he could view coldly in black and white, a simple case of fight or flight!

"Okay. I'll not ask again," Sir Hector looked relieved to have asked and survived the question.

"So, back to business then - we've worked out a suitable history for you," Sir Hector said impassively. "We've come up with your cover name, Jakob. You are a Swedish citizen as you speak Swedish along with several others fluently. You are wanted in Sweden and the US for computer hacking crimes against banking institutions but the authorities do not have any images of you." He opened a file on screen. "You're making your way to the UK. We've kept it simple with everything you need for your background. The file has been emailed in the usual encrypted format. Read it. Naturally, you now have a new Swedish bank account with funds deposited. You're willing to pay any price to get into the UK, no questions asked."

Dillon felt, as usual, as if a large wave was rolling over him, tossing him over the sand onto the beach. "When do I leave?"

"There's a flight out of city airport to Florence at 13.35 today. Your booking has been made, you'll find that old canvas travel holdall of yours with my assistant. I had Miss Young bring it over for you. She packed what she thought you might need."

"Did she, well that must have been a new experience for her. What about my Glock?"

"What about it?"

"I'm not going into this assignment unarmed."

Sir Hector removed his glasses and buffed the lenses with the corner of his handkerchief and replaced them again, he looked up, "I'll arrange for one of our people to meet you down there. Let Miss Young know on your way out."

Dillon stood. The briefing had come to an end.

"Dillon."

"Yes, Sir Hector."

"On this assignment I want you to chase the trail, hunt down those involved and find out what they're scheming. You have been authorised at the highest level of government to take care of all loose ends. Those you find to be involved should be identified and taken care of. Do I make myself clear?"

"Yes, I understand." Dillon turned and started to walk out of the office.

"Oh, just one other thing, Dillon."

"What's that, Sir Hector?"

"Use that Glock wisely."

Dillon closed the door gently. Outside Phoebe Young was sitting at her desk, looking alluring.

"What's with the look?"

"You survived the Sir Hector Blackwood experience! I hope you don't mind but I was sent over to your apartment to pack a bag for you."

"So, I hear. Thank you."

"That place of yours by the way is fantastic." She quickly realised her over familiarity and looked suddenly coy.

Dillon smiled at her and said in fluent Swedish. "Tack. Skulle du vilja middag när jag kommer tillbaka?"

She stared at him in amazement. "Thank you. I would love to have dinner with you when you return."

"You speak Swedish."

"Enough to get by. Now what is it you want sent down to Florence in the diplomatic bag?"

"A Glock 20 with at least ten fully loaded clips and a shoulder holster for a left hander." He picked up his holdall and while she was still writing, he left.

Chapter 3

Florence Italy
And
Guernsey
Channel Islands
April

A strikingly beautiful woman sitting by the window of the intercity train, sun light streamed into the carriage highlighting lustrous dark brown hair. She was somewhere in her mid-thirties, no more than forty. A flawless complexion and chestnut brown eyes set off to perfection by the vivid scarf swathed around her neck and shoulders, held Dillon's gaze.

Dillon had seen her only once before during the twelve-hour train ride from Florence to Paris and now here she was again on this train to Brest. He walked on through to the buffet car ordered a coffee, picked out a newspaper from the rack and sat facing the door.

He was still there fifteen minutes later, reading that day's edition of Le Figaro when she came into the carriage. She looked at Dillon nervously as she walked up to the counter and ordered a coffee. Dillon stole a sneaky look at this enigmatic lady. She didn't fit the bill of a fugitive or a refugee fleeing a war zone. Wearing expensive skin-tight designer denim jeans, brown leather riding style boots and a soft tan coloured leather jacket. The colourful scarf was now draped casually around her shoulders showing off shoulder length hair. Turning around, she picked up the coffee and walked off in the direction of the forward carriages.

* * *

Brest
France

Dillon got up out of his seat as the intercity train from Paris pulled into the station at Brest. He slung the canvas hold all over his shoulder. Stepped onto the platform and momentarily glanced around taking in the smell of heat, fumes and people that can only be felt in train terminals. In amongst the throng of people getting off the train he spotted her again. She was standing further along the platform with a bag at her feet looking edgy, constantly checking her mobile phone. After waiting around for ten minutes Dillon received a text message.

Welcome to Brest, Jakob. Leave the station now by the main entrance and once outside the building, wait. We will collect you in five minutes.

Dillon looked around the platform, picked up his holdall and walked out through the main entrance with everyone else. He lit a cigarette and leaned against the wall, waiting as instructed.

A blue minibus pulled up to the kerb, its body work battered and covered in dust. The driver was somewhere in his late twenties wearing a black beanie hat and a grubby oversized hoody; he motioned Dillon into the minibus. Not surprisingly the dark brown-haired woman was there she looked intently at Dillon as he sat on the bench-seat behind the driver.

"Where are you taking us?" Dillon asked.

The driver carried on driving and smoking his cheroot but didn't answer.

"Hey. I said where are you taking us?" Dillon repeated.

The driver glanced up in to the rear-view mirror his eyes sullen.

"You'll know when we get there, mister. Now chill-out, sit back and enjoy the ride, man."

Dillon let it go, turned in his seat and introduced himself to his travelling companion.

* * *

The minibus travelled out of Brest on a main road towards the east for fifteen miles, crossing a bridge over a wide estuary. Passing through picturesque countryside to a small harbour at

L'Auberlach where a boat was waiting for them.

During the short journey Dillon discovered her name. He was travelling with Camille De Santi. She wasn't very talkative but Dillon could tell she came from money; her manner went hand in glove with his theory. Her English was without fault, most likely due to the public schools in England where her parents had sent her. The minibus slowed as it travelled towards a small harbour stopping when they ran out of road.

* * *

Getting out of the minibus they were led straight to the jetty where the boat was moored. Liam Finnegan was leaning on the side wearing a black reefer jacket and grubby beige coloured trousers at least a size too big there were held up with a wide leather belt. The buckle of which was in the shape of a pair of eagle's wings. Dillon eyed the big Irishman suspiciously from the quayside, who looked at Dillon and sneered contemptuously.

Camille De Santi went aboard and Dillon followed closely behind her. Finnegan looked even more repulsive close up as he was unshaven and by the smell of alcohol, body odour and cigarette's, obviously hadn't washed in a week. He walked in front of them towards the cabin; Camille De Santi hesitated fractionally before she followed closely behind Dillon.

Finnegan walked through the day to the sleeper cabins. He stopped at the first door and opened it.

"This will be your quarters." Finnegan gestured for Camille De Santi to enter the tiny cabin.

She stepped inside and Finnegan closed and locked the door. He looked directly at Dillon, willing him to make a smart comment but he remained silent and shrugged. Why should it bother him, he had more important things to ponder?

* * *

Liam Finnegan had been born of indeterminate parentage in Belfast fifty-eight years earlier. His mother was of Irish origin but his father had been an English soldier stationed there during the conflict. Finnegan was a disgrace to both nationalities. He had followed the sea his life and yet his right to a master's ticket was uncertain, to say the least. But he possessed other darker qualities in abundance that suited his life perfectly.

"You're next door to the woman." Finnegan opened the door and stepped back.

Dillon stepped inside the small cabin. Finnegan went to close the door and lock it but hadn't expected the response he got. Dillon's hand went to the Irishman's throat, the grip just tight enough, pinning him against the wooden panelling.

"Now you listen to me. I'm paying to get to the England and I expect to be treated with respect. You hear me?"

Finnegan nodded his understanding.

Dillon released him. Finnegan leaned forward doubled up, rubbing his throat and gasping for air. "Bastard, you could have killed me!"

"Trust me, if I'd wanted to kill you. You'd be dead. Now unlock the lady's door and fuck off and do your job." Dillon's said in a perfect Swedish accent.

Finnegan unlocked the door to Camille De Santi's cabin, gave Dillon a sullen sideways look and went back up the companionway to the bridge.

Dillon knocked on the cabin door and waited a moment before entering. He found Camille De Santi sitting on the narrow bunk with her head in her hands.

He leaned against the wooden panelling and waited for her sobbing to subside.

"You needn't be scared." Dillon softly spoke the words.

"Scared - why should I be scared Jakob?"

"Well, we're on this stinking old tub with a captain who most likely would sell his grandmother for a bottle of rum. To think he's taking us across the English Channel, that will take us through the busiest shipping lanes in the world. Even I'm worried by the prospect of that - especially with that drunken Finnegan at the wheel!"

"What can we do?"

"Nothing specific, but he's definitely not to be trusted."

"How long before we get to England?"

"Assuming that this old rot box will turn 25 knots or better I'd guess at best eight hours but if the tides against us it could be ten hours. It depends on how good a skipper Finnegan is!"

"Did you know they're picking up another passenger on

route in the Channel Islands?"

"No. How do you know this?"

"While I was waiting in the minibus, I overheard the driver talking on his mobile phone in Spanish. He repeated, the Russian was on the island."

"Interesting! What else did he say?"

"Nothing."

"Lock your door and don't open it for anyone except me. You do understand that your life is in danger?"

"Why should it be? I paid one hundred thousand Euros' to these people to get me to England safely."

"So, did I. But these people cannot be trusted and If we run into any trouble, they'll most likely kill us to save their own miserable skins. So be alert and stay on guard."

* * *

Guernsey
British Channel Islands

They reached Guernsey four hours after they had left the small harbour near Brest. It was getting dark when Finnegan slowed the Tide Runner to negotiate the rocks lurking just below the surface of the water.

Dillon had gone to his cabin earlier and was on the narrow bunk staring up at the flaking paint on the ceiling. It was nothing more than floating scrap. The skipper was dubious, the bedding was damp and unlaundered and it was grim.

Using the intelligence obtained by Interpol, Dillon had approached Finnegan in a bar in Lavorno located on the coast seventy-five kilometres south-west of Florence. Dillon had watched Liam Finnegan enter the bar and had followed him in five minutes later. He flashed a large wad of one-hundred Euro notes at the bartender and that had set the Irishman's eyes gleaming.

Dillon got into bar-room conversation with Finnegan, telling him that he was trying to get into England but couldn't use any of the conventional methods. He had not told him the whole story, especially not about the Cyber-criminal element of his fabricated history. He had decided to allow him to discover that for himself. The greed of this Irishman would be enough to gain his attention and interest to check his story out.

Finnegan had instructed Dillon to wait in the bar for him until he returned. An hour later he came back and sat opposite Dillon. Finnegan swallowed the story. For one hundred thousand Euros a safe passage was guaranteed. First by train to Paris then another to Brest where he boarded the Tide Runner to be taken across the Channel to England.

The fabricated history that Sir Hector had created had been successful. For the money, Dillon would be taken to Brest where he'd board Finnegan's boat to cross the Channel. And then landed illegally on the Dorset coast and sent on his way with transport to take him to a safe house.

* * *

Since boarding the boat Dillon had kept the Glock safely holstered under his jacket. He was surprised that the Irishman had not tried to relieve him of his cash and then thrown him overboard. Finnegan looked as if he'd sell his sister on the street given the opportunity.

There was a knock at his cabin door and Dan Lacroix, Finnegan's first mate spoke from outside the door.

"Captain Finnegan wants to see you up-top."

"Tell him I'll be up in five minutes."

"He said now!"

Dillon opened the door, staring coldly at Dan Lacroix - making the first mate awkward in his presence.

"Tell him five minutes."

Dillon went to the day cabin.

"So, Jakob, we are making a short stop."

"Where are we?

"Questions, questions, its questions all the time with you, isn't it? But if it helps, we are just off the coast of Guernsey."

"If you don't ask you don't find out, Captain Finnegan."

"Very true, now you've paid fifty thousand Euros' for your passage so far. It's time for you to transfer twenty–five thousand Euros into the same account."

Dillon used his smart-phone to transfer the money.

"Done - now what happens? Dillon demanded.

"You go back to your cabin and let me do my job. I'll have my first mate bring you and the lady coffee and sandwiches shortly."

"Is anyone else coming on-board?"

Finnegan looked round at Dillon. "That's my business," he snapped. "You ask too many questions for my liking, Jakob."

"I like to know who I'm travelling with Captain. I'm paying a large sum of money to you and your friends to get me to England. I don't want that jeopardised."

"So, you say, Jakob. But you needn't be worried. Everything has been thought through, I assure you, even the unexpected."

Dillon had made his point. It was futile to press Finnegan any further at this time. He went back to his cabin and sent Sir Hector an encrypted update by email.

On board the Tide Runner approaching Guernsey. Background checks for Captain Liam Finnegan and first mate Daniel Lacroix required. One other passenger - Camille De Santi, possibly Argentinian but could be Italian.

Finnegan to make stop somewhere on the island. Suggest tracking satellite made available.

End of message.

JD

Something about Camille De Santi was nagging at the back of Dillon's mind. He didn't know what it was - she just didn't fit the profile of someone who was running from something or someone. The designer clothing, the voice and fluency of English she spoke, it didn't sit well with Dillon. His guts told him to keep his guard up around her.

The Tide Runner slowed to a stop, the swell gently rocking the old boat that was now drifting with the tide. Dillon could hear voices above and then the sound of an outboard engine starting. They were going to pick up whoever it was waiting on a beach. He withdrew the Glock from its holster, checked there was a round in the chamber and re-holstered the weapon.

One hour later the Tide Runner's powerful diesel engines were started, they were under way once again. Dillon could hear footsteps above him and laughter coming from the main cabin.

* * *

One Mile off the coast of Dorset
Poole Harbour
UK

A knock on the cabin door and the first mate informed him that Captain Finnegan would like to see him up-top. Dillon got up off the bunk and opened the door, following Dan Lacroix up the companionway.

"So, Jakob, we are nearing our destination. When we get close to the coast, you will transfer to the dinghy with Lacroix and be taken ashore." Finnegan looked warily at Dillon. "I don't like you, Jakob, or whatever your name is."

"Lucky me! But then, I don't care much for you either, Finnegan." Dillon said bluntly accentuating the clipped Swedish accent with little emotion. "Where do I go once I'm ashore?" Dillon held the Irishman's gaze.

"Lacroix will get you ashore at a point of the harbour that's easily accessible and security thin on the ground. No one will stop you when you pass through the gate of the boat yard. Someone will meet you and ask if you're looking for taxi."

"What about the woman?" Dillon asked.

"What about her?" Finnegan demanded his smile fading.

"Nothing in particular, I thought she might be leaving with me."

"You are mistaken." Finnegan rose to his feet, wiped his face with a grubby handkerchief and held out his hand. "I might not like you Jakob but I wish you luck on your way."

Dillon smiled at Finnegan and Lacroix, ignored the outstretched hand and went back to collect his holdall and trench coat. When he came up on deck, he went straight to Lacroix waiting in the dingy.

* * *

The dinghy raced through the fading light of evening towards the harbour entrance. Dan Lacroix slowed the inflatable craft where the channel narrowed and Shell Bay was linked to the Sandbanks Peninsular by the chain-link ferry. Passing through without drama they entered the world's largest natural harbour. The Tide Runner followed a few minutes later.

Dan Lacroix steered a course around the south west shore of Brownsea Island and through the channel of White Ground Lake towards Ramshorn Lake. As the harbour widened they gathered speed towards the shore.

Dillon shuffled nearer to Lacroix and over the noise asked him where he was putting him ashore.

"We're heading for Lake Marina. Captain Finnegan's cousin works there and will see you get to your collection point."

* * *

Finnegan was talking to his cousin at the boatyard on the ship to shore radio.

"The Swede has a considerable amount of cash on him. I suggest you relieve him of it; get your two sons on to it, they should be able to handle it. He won't make any fuss. Everyone is looking for him in England and United States as well as Sweden and Germany."

Finnegan poured himself a large tumbler of rum, which he drank slowly. When he looked outside the rain was beating down heavily. He moved along the companionway to the woman's cabin, knocked and went to enter. The door was locked.

"It's Captain Finnegan, miss. Can you please unlock the door? We've arrived in England. A moment later he could hear movement from inside the cabin and the click of the lock releasing. He barged in, pushing the door open violently.

She turned from the bunk to face him, looking strangely calm. There was something close to alarm on her face but she made a visible effort and smiled.

"Captain Finnegan. It is time, then?"

"It most definitely is," Finnegan said, moving with astonishing swiftness for a drunk. He grabbed her tightly from behind, groping her as she tried to get free, her elbow catching him hard in the ribs. He hit her hard across the side of her face with the flat of his hand. Pushed her down across the bunk flipped her over and flung himself on top of her.

* * *

Darren and Wayne Cooper, twin brothers and boat yard labourers. They both wore the same Lacoste tracksuits, had the same jet-black hair cut short back and sides and swarthy gypsy tan. Wayne hurried along the pontoon and paused at the security gate to listen. There was no sound, no outboard motor in the distance only the gentle lapping of the water against the floating platform. Darren unlocked the metal gate, ensuring that it was left ajar.

They walked up the driveway between workshops and the dry-docked boats, to the carpark where the camera coverage was patchy and the lighting poor. Darren instructed Wayne to wait in the shadows until he saw the man heading their way.

Darren moved to the other side of the car park and concealed himself by a metal shipping container. He stood in the shadows, lit a cigarette and waited for Dillon to appear. A moment later they heard the metal gate open and then close, gravel crunching underfoot.

Dillon smelt the familiar whiff of cigarette smoke drifting on the night air as he walked towards the main gate. He stopped walking and moved quietly into the darkness alongside a large boat undergoing work on timber supports. He felt an overwhelming sense of foreboding as he stood watching and listening. Slowing his breathing, he could feel the adrenaline rushing through his body heightening his senses as he prepared for the inevitable to happen.

Darren broke his cover moments later and crouching low dashed across the car park to join his brother.

"What's happened to him, where did he go?" Darren demanded in a low panicked whisper.

The tall swarthy boat yard labourers appeared, walking gingerly down the driveway. As they drew level Dillon moved out of the shadows. Tapped Darren lightly on the shoulder and as he spun round, raised a knee into his testicles. He sagged to the ground and Dillon stepped over the writhing body smiling at Wayne.

"What kept you, big man?"

Wayne moved in fast, the nine-inch blade of a serrated hunting knife in his right-hand glinting in the overhead lights. His feet were kicked from beneath him and he hit the ground with a heavy thud, breath leaving his lungs with a grunt. He started to get up and Dillon seized his right wrist, twisted the arm around his back and up in a direction it was never intended to go. Wayne screamed as his shoulder dislocated and muscle ripped as Dillon ran him headfirst into a stack of oil drums.

Darren was back up on his feet and bent double being sick. Dillon grabbed him by the collar of his shirt and heaved him upright, the barrel of the Glock pushed hard against his throat. "Who ordered you to attack me?" Dillon demanded aggressively.

Darren glared at Dillon who hit him hard across the side of his face with the butt of the pistol. The boat yard labourer groaned. Asking again with the threat of another dose of pain got the information he wanted.

"No! Don't do that again." Darren held his hands up defensively. "It was Finnegan, he used the ship to shore radio to let our dad know that you were carrying cash. We had to wait for you and rob you as you came up from the water."

"Where is the woman now?"

"Finnegan always keeps the women back for himself. Dirty old bastard..."

Dillon's punch left Darren unconscious on the ground next to Wayne. He sprinted back to the marina, only faltering to negotiate the metal security gate. He moved along the pontoon and jumped off into an old small powerboat that looked easy to hot-wire the ignition. Moments later he was leaving the marina and once in open water, opened the throttle and raced towards the Tide Runner at anchor on the far side of the harbour.

* * *

Camille De Santi struggled with Finnegan, scratched, punched and kicked out as he ripped open her blouse and forced her onto the bunk half naked. His filthy hands pawed her body; prising her legs apart roughly.

Relaxing the tension in her muscles she feigned helplessness as he roughly parted her legs but he hadn't reckoned on the kick to the side of his head coming. Finnegan was stunned briefly but came back at her.

She landed the heel of her boot in his stomach, he was strong and aggressive but she managed to manoeuvre back into a sitting position slapping him in anger with all her strength. He grunted as one of her blows caught him flat across the side of his face. The punch he threw at her was much more brutal, cutting her across the cheekbone with the force of the blow.

"I'm going to take that fucking superior smug look right off your face, missy," he spat. "You're going to get what's been coming to you since stepping on to this boat."

He stood up, beads of sweat rolling down his unshaven face - unzipped his trousers and started to loosen off his belt.

The door swung open and Dillon stepped stood in the open doorway. He held the Glock casually in his left hand by his side and had the devil in his eye.

Finnegan swung round and Dillon released the safety catch.

"You really are a nasty bastard, aren't you, Finnegan?"

Finnegan took a step forward. Dillon brought his left arm up so quickly that the Irishman only knew what was happening after the pistol butt had hit him full in the face. His nose shattered, bone and tissue broke and tore, blood flowed freely.

He stumbled back falling across the bunk. Camille De Santi didn't waste any time and hit hard between the legs with the toe of her boot and then moved to Dillon, who put an arm around her.

"Let me guess. You're entering England through the back door because you're wanted for crimes against the state."

"Perhaps you're right, perhaps not."

"Both in the same boat, then. How much did he charge you?"

"He took fifty thousand Euros in cash from me in Florence as a down payment and another twenty-five thousand when we reached England, payable by bank transfer."

"Did he, now?" Dillon hauled Finnegan up on to his feet and shoved him towards the door. "Get your things together and wait for me at the stern rail. This piece of scum and I have things to discuss."

Dillon pushed Finnegan up the companionway and into the day cabin; the captain turned angrily, blood on his face. "You won't get away with this."

Dillon hit him across the face twice in quick succession with the gun, knocking him to the floor. He squatted beside him and said amiably. "Get the lady's money, I haven't got much time."

Finnegan produced a key from his trouser pocket, dragged

himself to a metal locker under the control console and opened it. Behind the metal door was a safe, Finnegan placed his palm on the biometric plate and the heavy door swung open. He tossed a large bundle of Euro notes across to Dillon.

"Oh, come now, Finnegan. You can do better than that, surely."

Dillon pushed him to one side. Reached into the safe and picked up four thick bundles of fifty-pound notes and stuffed them into his jacket pockets with a satisfying smile.

"I hope you learn a valuable lesson by this, Finnegan. I should put a bullet in your miserable head but I'm suddenly feeling generous. So today you live." He tapped him on the forehead with the barrel of the Glock. "It's been a pleasure teaching you this lesson and now if you wouldn't mind, how do we get to this safe house?"

"There's a black Range Rover parked in the boat yard car park. The driver will take you to a pub called The Quay Inn on Wareham quay. Ask for Garrick."

"If you're setting me up again, I'll be back," Dillon said coolly, not believing a word the Irishman was saying.

Finnegan could barely whisper as he tried to sit upright. "It's the truth, I'm not lying."

Dillon stood.

"But I'll have my day, you know." Finnegan said sneeringly.

Dillon kicked the Irishman in the ribs, pushing him up against the forward bulkhead. He didn't want to kill him, that could wait, just break bones.

Outside Camille De Santi was waiting at the stern rail for Dillon as he came out. She stood looking cold, anxious and bruised. Her face framed by a scarf around her head and now wearing a long Burberry rain coat.

"I was beginning to get worried," she said in her soft Latin voice.

"No need." He handed her two of the bundles of fifty-pound notes he had taken from Finnegan. "I think these are yours."

She looked at him with wonder.

"Who are you?"

"A friend," he said gently and picked up her travel bag.

"Now let's get moving. I think it would be healthier in the long run."

He jumped down into the dinghy, taking her arm as she stepped down and sat on the bench seat beside him.

Chapter 4

Poole Harbour
Dorset
April

Dillon steered a course through the rain and darkness across the harbour, passing Poole Quay and onwards towards the Sandbanks Peninsular.

"Where are we going?" Camille De Santi shouted over the noise of the outboard engine.

"Over there," Dillon pointed to the far side of the harbour, "somewhere safe!"

They passed the public slipway at Baiter Park on their left. Then the Parkstone Yacht Club marina, following the buoys marking the channel round the bay until they reached the Royal Motor Yacht Club on the peninsular. Dillon slowed the dinghy to a crawl as they passed by the private jetties of luxury waterside properties until he veered towards one of them, killed the outboard engine and came alongside the wooden jetty, bowline secured, he jumped out of the small craft and helped Camille De Santi up onto the landing-stage.

They walked towards the house, tripping the security perimeter laser line. Powerful lights lit up the grounds, blinding them both for a moment. They stood at the edge of the large expanse of lawn - waiting. To one side of the main house a door opened, followed by the sound of dogs and heavy footsteps coming towards them. Camille stepped back behind Dillon and the silhouette of a man carrying an assault rifle became visible as he came to within twenty feet of where they were standing.

The figure halted, the barrel of the Heckler and Koch G36 pointing at them. The two small dogs ran towards Dillon.

Dillon stepped forward; crouched and made a fuss of the

two French Bulldogs who snuffled and snorted as they made a fuss of him.

"It's been a long time, Rumple." Dillon said looking up at the older man.

"Too long sir. It's great to see you. Mrs Rumple has the kettle on, sir."

"That sounds an excellent idea, Rumple. How are these two doing since coming here?"

"They've settled in well. That was a kind thing you did, bringing them to Dorset. They love their walks on the beach every day."

"Well, I couldn't resist them Rumple. With the death of Lillian Krasner, the two of them were heading for the local rescue centre, or worse. When this assignment is over, I'll take them up to Scotland with me for the summer."

Camille De Santi looked on in bewilderment at the conversation Dillon was having with Rumple but remained silent.

Rumple led them through well-tended grounds. The sound of the rain falling and water lapping against the jetty faded as they reached the main house.

"Mrs Rumple, it's good to see you." Dillon said giving her a hug. He had worked many times with the Rumples. They were once again caretaking his house that used to belong to Charlie Hart. Now they were to help him on this assignment.

"It's always good to see you, sir. How long has it been since we worked together?"

"Too long Mrs R."

"And who is this we have here?"

"Camille De Santi, meet Mr & Mrs Rumple."

Introductions done, Dillon had to find out who was Camille De Santi. He didn't know if he could trust her or would she comprehend the reality of her involvement. He led her to the elevator and selected level three, the door opened and they stepped out into a tropical garden under a roof of glass. Filtered lighting bounced surreal shadows around, over and below the large exotic plants. Moments later, Mrs Rumple arrived with a tray of coffee and sandwiches. Camille De Santi sank into one of the massive beanbags as Dillon poured the coffee.

"You're wondering…"

"This," she waved her hand around the roof-top room. "makes me wonder what you might be into."

"Yes - you're wondering. I appreciate your position but I'm wondering too Camille." Dillon stood up and walked around the garden. "Who are you?"

"You know who I am." Her tone was indignant.

"Only what you've told me. But your story doesn't sit right, you're too confident, most likely more used to causing conflict than running from it and that little show with Finnegan on the boat. You were toying with him. I'd make a guess you're trained in martial arts for sure but you played the victim, something you are not."

"You make assumptions, don't you and you're not Swedish, although you speak the language. You're far too English looking."

Dillon smiled at her comments but remained silent for a moment, deciding to leave it for the time being.

"Come with me. I want to show something so unusual that it will take your breath away."

She nodded. They walked back to the first floor and walked to the far end of a wide landing.

The gallery vestibule doubled as an air lock, with a second door made from one-inch thick Armorlite Steel on the opposite side of the small space. Eight electromagnetic locking shoot-bolts along four edges fitted with anti-tamper contact points between the door and its frame connected these to the main security network. There were no windows, and the room had its own computer-controlled air-conditioning, independent of the main house. The air felt cool, the temperature constant, the paintings maintained in pristine condition. Recessed spotlights and concealed sound speakers around the gallery controlled by a remote unit inside the air-lock.

Dillon watched as Camille walked around the private collection of priceless art and artifacts.

"I purchased this house from the son of Charlie Hart. A criminal I'd been investigating, who it turned out was a likable bloke and we discovered had much in common."

"Where is this man now?"

"He shot himself. Out there by the water. The police were here to arrest him and the thought of being locked up for the rest of his life..."

"How very sad, for a life to end in that way but why are you telling me this?"

Dillon led her by the arm to the centre of the labyrinthine room.

A round pedestal made of black onyx stood on its own surrounded by priceless works of art by Vermeer, Picasso, Matisse and other renowned artists. Placed on the polished top was a life size skull carved out of a solid piece of natural quartz crystal.

Dillon at once sensed her being seduced by its exquisiteness, by the mystery of why it existed. She moved around it, eyes transfixed, marveled at the Mayan craftsmanship. Even the teeth were so life like, smooth contours of the cheekbones and the way the jaw fitted into the cranium. The question, Dillon knew she was asking herself, how.

"Mayan's were an indigenous people who lived a simple life deep in the South American jungle who sculpted something so accomplished as this skull, so perfect. But that's part of its allure."

Dillon paused for effect before saying. "If the Mayan's created the skull, they had to use copper rods and hand bows. It took immense patience to sand the natural block of quartz using a mixture of river sand and water. Several generations of effort worked to achieve the finished sculpture, and that's assuming the quartz didn't shatter along the way. How dear old Charlie Hart had come by the skull was still a mystery. Not even Charlie's son Daniel knew where it came from."

"This is the most stunning thing I've ever seen." Camille stood face to face with the skull.

"If you're interested..."

"Please, go on."

"Well, the myth that surrounds the skull is that it's one of thirteen crystal skulls. Some have come to the surface in South America over the years by archaeologists. There's been huge interest in the skulls from scientists who have investigated deep into the fabric of the quartz with the latest technology. There have been eminent psychics who have come into contact with them. They reported the same thing, the skulls showed them that each one holds information of our world. The past, the present and the future and that they have the power to deliver both good and evil to the world. Should the thirteen ever come together, it would give whoever had them in their possession an invincible power. Whether any of that is fact or fiction is anyone's guess." Dillon smiled.

"This is the most amazing thing I've ever seen."

"Yes, it never loses its appeal." Dillon walked around the skull and stopped in front of it

"Camille, you still haven't answered my question. Who are you and why were you on that boat?"

"What's to say you're not a trafficker?"

"Because Camille, I'm not a trafficker!" Dillon held her stare for a moment. "My name isn't Jakob and I'm not a Swedish computer hacker. It's Jake Dillon and I work for British Intelligence. Those two-people downstairs are the best facilitators and house-keepers in the business. Mr Rumple is a former Special Forces operative and Mrs R has worked for the British Secret Service for over forty years. Together they watch my back and get whatever I need while on assignment."

"I guessed as much. Not that you were spooks but you might have been undercover somethings."

"I've never thought of myself as an undercover something!" Dillon smiled. "So, tell me, what's your real name?"

Camille looked at Dillon, still unsure but feeling she had nothing to lose given her present state of affairs. "My real name is Camille but not De Santi, De Rosa. I work for the anti-terrorism unit of Interpol in Rome. I am a senior investigator with a PhD in forensic science. As for my little show with Finnegan on the boat - you're right. It would have been easy to have broken his neck but I didn't want to blow my cover with his paymasters who are our primary aim. If they'd found him dead, they'd have assumed that I'd been the one to have killed him given his past with the female passengers.

We've been investigating these people for well over a year now. So far, we have discovered that they are careful, operating as individual cells of three or four people. Our tech guys have picked up email chatter between terrorist organisations and a computer terminal in northern France and another in Guernsey. We decrypted a few of the messages but they change the cypher daily making it difficult for us. They move their location every day and route their emails all over the planet to evade being tracked.

The messages we have intercepted relate to known terrorists moving around. But anyone who can pay their way in Euros, Dollars or Sterling can enter England without the authorities knowing. My cover was that I'd murdered a high-ranking government official and had to get out of Italy as fast as possible."

"Interpol field agents have a support team, where's yours?"

"My support team were on my tail from the time I left Florence and were close by until we arrived in Brest. When that beaten up old van picked me up, they had to hang back. When we boarded the Tide Runner, the French authorities should have had a pursuit boat ready and waiting offshore. Their sole purpose was to pick them up once they knew the location. It never appeared, and that's when they lost visual contact but I sent off a text before we sailed and another when we stopped at Guernsey. The last time I messaged them was when we arrived in Poole harbour. They will arrive in the UK tomorrow once the relevant authorisation comes through for them to work on British soil."

"We should wait for them to contact you then. For tonight, I've asked Mrs R to make up one of the guest suites for you."

"That's great. A good night's sleep would be nice."

Mrs R appeared and showed Camille to her room. Dillon returned to his study on the ground floor in the round library room. He locked the door and went straight to his desk, opened a drawer and pressed the concealed button just behind the top rail of the unit. The panelling parted to expose a narrow stairwell that spiralled to a secret bunker. As Dillon entered the stairwell, he closed the panelling behind him.

He descended the eighteen flagstone steps to the bottom. Warm dry air from the air De-humidifier and conditioning unit met him as he entered the underground bunker. The lighting was modern as was the computer linked to a screen on the wall and another inset into the granite work surface of an island unit. The server started within seconds and multi touch-screens illuminated with images and menus that Dillon arranged and chose with the flick of a hand from one screen to another. A moment later the secure link connected.

"Good evening Mr Dillon."

"Good evening Sir Hector."

"Mr & Mrs Rumple are now with you?"

"Yes."

"Okay, be brief. I'm having dinner with the PM and she doesn't tolerate lateness."

"The Italian woman I told you was on the boat with me, her name isn't Camille De Santi, it's De Rosa. She works for Interpol out of their Rome office."

"So, what of it, we knew this. We spoke to the Italians earlier today, and they informed us she was heading our way. But the question is, Dillon - can she be of use to your investigation?"

"That's what I was wondering."

"What is your next move?"

"Rumple has chartered a helicopter which I intend to fly to Guernsey in the morning. I believe Finnegan, the skipper of The Tide Runner anchored near to a cove on the northern side of the island to collect something or someone. I'm not sure which but I want to take a look and see what we can find out from the locals."

"Okay Dillon. Keep me up speed at all times, understood?"

"No problem."

"I think Camille De Rosa could be useful to the investigation but there's an Interpol support team on their way here to babysit her."

"And you don't want them to join your party, eh? Okay, I'll see to it they're sent back to Rome. Any other business, Dillon?"

"No, I don't think so Sir Hector. Enjoy your dinner."

The video link was severed and Dillon smiled to himself. Pouring a single malt whisky, he stood by the window overlooking the harbour – planning his next move.

* * *

The next morning, Camille De Rosa came to find Dillon sitting with Rumple and Mrs R at the breakfast table.

"Good morning Camille. Sleep well?" Dillon asked.

"Like a baby, thank you. Has there been any news of my support team?"

"Yes, I received a message earlier. They've not turned up on this side of the channel. But Sir Hector Black, my boss has spoken to your head of department in Rome. They both agree it would be in the best interest of the investigation if you and I work together. Instead of on opposite sides."

Camille looked at Dillon and then at her phone. She walked out of the room. Calling her boss in Rome after a few moments of fast Italian conversation she hung up and went back into the breakfast room to re-join the others.

"So, it's arranged – we're working together Mr Dillon!"

Chapter 5

The rain from the day before had cleared, giving way to an early morning sky of dazzling blue with only a scattering of white cloud. Over breakfast, Dillon discussed with the Rumples the brief for enquiries they were to make while he was away. To find out who was who: apart from the ruffians he'd had the run-in with and their uncle at the boat yard, who was involved in the trafficking ring at the Dorset end? In particular to find this man named Garrick in Wareham. If they located him and felt he was a threat to the on-going investigation to have him arrested but first call Phoebe Young, Sir Hector's personal assistant so she could arrange everything.

He'd agreed with Camille that she'd be ready to leave within the hour. Dillon made his way to the bunker below the study. He placed his hand on the biometric reader and a moment later the false panel in the stone wall moved round to expose an equipped armoury with an impressive array of sophisticated military weaponry.

Dillon treated the hardware with reverence. They had saved his life on numerous occasions. A Russian Special Forces ADS assault rifle was the first weapon Dillon picked out of the rack. Designed for use underwater, firing seven-hundred rounds per minute at a range of up to twenty-five metres. That might come in handy, he thought. Next to it was a Magpul FMG-9 submachine gun. Made of lightweight polymer that could reduce to the size of a rectangular block, the size of a laptop battery. He placed that in his holdall.

Dillon had a favourite handgun with an unequalled uniqueness, the Armatix Ip1 pistol that required his fingerprint-enabled smart-watch to be within twenty-five centimetres of it to fire. Dillon stood for a moment toying with the weapon in his hands; he took it with him along with his Glock.

He met Camille in the ground floor hallway and led her

outside to the south lawn. They both looked; overhead the pulsing beat of helicopter rotors approaching and a moment later the black outline of a Bell 505 JetRanger X came into view. Camille stood motionless looking up, her perfect ponytail lifted by the downdraft of the rotors, hair whipping around her face as the helicopter descended onto the lawn. She smoothed it back with one hand to regain order. Dillon smiled at her many attempts that were failing. The uniformed pilot stepped out of the sleek black cabin, stooping under the rotor's blades as he walked straight over to Dillon. They talked for a minute before Rumple came and accompanied him into the main house for breakfast and to await his ride back to the airport.

Dillon motioned for Camille to follow him to the JetRanger, her hair still being blown around from the idling rotor-blades as she walked across the lawn. He threw their bags into the rear of the cabin and they both climbed into the front seats. He handed her a headset. The effect was immediate with only minimal rotor noise entering the ear-phones.

"Strap yourself in tight; we don't want you falling out."

"Can you fly this helicopter?"

"I reckon it can't be that difficult but we'll soon find out!" He cast a sideward glance at her.

"You are kidding, right? So where are we going?"

Before Dillon could answer, Rumple's voice came over the radio comm.

"London has just confirmed the name at the top of the tree. I will send it through to your phone."

"Excellent work Rumple – thank London."

Dillon's smart phone vibrated in his jacket pocket. The name in the text was not familiar to him.

Mon, 09/04/2017]
Target:
ELLIOTT STARK

Dillon showed Camille the message before deleting it, she wasn't aware of Elliott Stark. He slipped his phone back into his jacket pocket and continued going through his pre-flight checks. Satisfied that everything was operating and warning lights were out he increased the power to lift the JetRanger into the air, hovering seven feet off the ground. He gazed through the cockpit to check there was nothing around to catch the blades on, radioed air-traffic control at Bournemouth and a moment later got the go ahead.

* * *

They circled once around Brownsea island before Dillon climbed to fifteen-hundred feet. He flew the JetRanger over the chain-link ferry and out towards open water, heading south-west on a sky of brilliant blue.

Dillon settled the JetRanger into a cruising speed of one-hundred and fifteen knots at an altitude of three thousand feet.

"You asked me where we were heading. Our first stop is Guernsey to where Finnegan picked up the mystery passenger; it could have been Elliott Stark, whom we never got to meet."

"How far is it to Guernsey?"

"From Poole, it's just over ninety-nine miles, which given our speed and altitude will take us fifty minute's flight time to get there."

"What do you expect to find?"

"Not what, Camille. But, who do I expect to find!" Dillon looked at her, the strain she'd been under during the past few days leaving her face.

She leaned back in her seat, head turned to look through her own reflection to the black heaving water, scarred and slashed with silver below them. She was an intelligent woman, Dillon decided. A sophisticated, elegant woman who chased organised criminal gangs around Europe. As an experienced field officer of Interpol, she was more than qualified and capable of looking after herself. He'd made the right decision working this assignment with Camille De Rosa with what she knew of the case.

Dillon adjusted their course and altitude as he took the JetRanger to two-thousand five-hundred feet above the English Channel as they started the approach to Guernsey.

* * *

They picked up a hire-car at Guernsey airport and drove up to where Finnegan had brought the Tide Runner to anchor on the north-west coast. Dillon parked the car at the top of a narrow road that twisted and turned down the hill to the harbour and hamlet. As they wandered towards the small harbour it was as if everyone had left. The small fisherman cottages looked deserted and there were no boats in the harbour, only small dinghies tied to their mooring buoys. When they reached the end of the quay Dillon spotted the only pub set back with wooden tables and chairs in the garden.

Alone at one of these tables was a wizened old grey-haired man sipping a pint of ale and holding a skinny roll-up between nicotine stained fingers. He had an air of indifference about him; even life itself and the pallor of his skin, coupled with his constant, repetitive coughing did not bode well for him.

"Excuse me; do you know if any of the skippers are interested in private charters?"

The old man puffed on his roll-up, exhaling a white plume of smoke out of the corner of his mouth and coughing. "Might, it depends see," he answered Dillon with a frigid civility, as if his attention was elsewhere.

"Depends on what?" Camille asked.

"What size boat you want and how much you're willing to pay for it, see."

Dillon looked around at the empty harbour and smiled to himself, asking. "Can I buy you another pint?"

"Why?"

"No reason, your glass is empty and I'd appreciate it if I could ask you about the boats that moor in this harbour!"

The craggy tanned face looked up at Dillon and smiled. "No harm in that, I suppose. Go on then, I'll have a pint of ale."

The pub stood back from the sea with a low stone wall protecting it from the harsh elements during the winter months. A wrought iron gate opened on to a gravel path that led to the main entrance. Over the years severe weather had taken its toll on the whitewashed elevations. Paint flaking and signs of damp near the ground which had turned the whitewash to a green, brown colour.

Dillon pushed open the scarred oak door, having to mind his head as he walked into the dim light of the public bar; Camille followed, stooping because of the low ceiling. Inside was pure gloom. Windows covered in a winter's worth of sea spray and grime filtered minimal light into a room straight out of the 1960's. The décor looked tired and shabby. As they walked into "The Mucky Duck', the man behind the bar looked at them.

The warmth inside from the open log fire felt good as Dillon and Camille moved towards the copper-topped bar. A middle-aged balding man wearing a black shirt with 'The Mucky Duck' with his name, Trevor, printed on the breast pocket stood behind the bar. He had one hand resting on top of the ale taps.

"What can I get for you folks?"

Dillon ordered two espresso coffees and a pint of ale for the old man sitting in the garden. The bartender pulled the pint of ale and poured the coffee into tiny espresso cups. While he paid the bill, Camille strolled outside to see if she could find out anything useful from the old man. Dillon leaned on the bar and made conversation with the bartender.

"I'm told it might be possible to charter a boat with a skipper around here?"

Trevor nodded as he poured a double measure of rum into a tumbler for himself. He looked up at Dillon with sullen eyes filled with suspicion.

"And who told you that, now?" He said the words with something resembling an Australian accent.

"Oh, it was the man at the hire-car desk. He mentioned it when we told him we were coming to this part of the island." Dillon lied.

"Well there might be a skipper wanting a trip out. Depends on where you want to go and what fishing you want."

His reaction was now more interesting and Dillon smiled. "We're spending a day, maybe two on the island before making our way to the UK. In fact, we are looking for a boat to take us across the Channel, if you can recommend anyone?"

"Not fishing, eh. Well you can catch the ferry to Poole, be

less money and most likely quicker."

"True, but we'd prefer a more discreet crossing." Dillon picked up his coffee and was about to walk outside, when he changed his mind and set the cat amongst the pigeons. "Do you know a captain Finnegan or Mr Elliott Stark?"

"Might do, during the season we get many people in here, see." He looked at Dillon, holding his gaze for a second while he wiped the bar top. After a moment, Dillon turned and stooping under the low ceiling beams, left the bar, glancing over his shoulder as he got to the door. He caught sight of the bartender moving through a swing door that led to the back of the building. Once outside, Dillon sat at the table opposite Camille.

"Where's the old man?"

"He didn't utter a word. Just sat there, sipping his pint. When I mentioned that pig Liam Finnegan he laughed, got up and walked off to one of those cottages."

"You've done a good job then." Dillon said.

"What? Are you taking the piss Dillon?"

"No – you misunderstand me, Camille. You see his actions speak volumes. It's the same reaction as that bartender. They know Finnegan and Stark and I'd say they're contacting them, right now.

"You could be right."

"There's no could be, agent De Rosa. Those men might make our job easier! We have to wait for a reaction, watch them and listen for anything that might prove to be of interest." Dillon stood up and peered through the doorway into the pub. The bartender had vanished.

"Stay here and keep alert. I'll only be a minute," Dillon told Camille and followed him.

He found himself in a deserted corridor. At the far end a notice pointed to the toilets. There was no sign of the bartender. Dillon moved forward and paused. A door to his left was ajar. The bartender stood with his back to the doorway. Talking in a low voice on the telephone, speaking Italian to whoever was at the other end of the phone line. Dillon remained in the corridor listening to the one-sided conversation he translated.

Trevor spoke with a low voice into the handset. "Hello, Mr Stark. Those two packages you lost on the last trip to Poole. Well they've turned up here. Yes, I can confirm that both fit the description you gave me, but one of them is giving me concern. I agree - looks dangerous. Okay I'll keep my eye on them for you. They're outside in the garden at the moment."

Dillon slipped out to Camille who was finishing her drink. "Your coffee must be cold by now."

"Never mind, we need to leave here."

"Is there a problem?"

"Not yet."

They walked out through the wrought iron gate and along a gravel path to the harbourside without glancing back at the pub. As they passed the fisherman's cottages they noticed the old man from outside the pub earlier. He was in a small dinghy sailing out of the harbour under the power of a noisy two-stroke outboard motor.

Something wasn't sitting well with Camille.

"What did that barman say to you?"

Dillon stopped walking and turning to her explained that he'd overheard Trevor the bartender talking on the phone to Elliott Stark. He was talking about them both being on the island.

"What do you suggest we do?"

"First, I will send an update back to London and copy Rumple. Then we go check out the surroundings, followed by lunch back at 'The Mucky Duck'. And then we wait for events to take their natural course."

* * *

As time passed, people came, walkers loaded with backpacks wearing waterproof clothing and a few sailing boats coming into the harbour. Dillon had chosen a table inside with a view of the front door, the bar and by a window overlooking the harbour.

It was half an hour later when a black pick-up truck turned onto the harbourside and parked outside the pub.

Dillon nudged Camille while watching as the brawny shaven-headed driver got out and stood leaning against the driver's door. After a moment, a white van pulled up behind the pick-up truck. A man somewhere in his forties, wearing a military style field jacket got out and walked towards the pub.

Camille reacted at once. "What a rough evil looking man."

"Appearances can be deceptive," Dillon commented.

"What do you mean? By the look of him he's been punched in the face too many times and most likely enjoyed it."

"True, he is an ugly looking devil." Dillon said without humour.

The man paused just inside the door, glancing around the room as if looking for someone in particular before approaching the bar and yet he had marked them. Dillon was sure of it. He ordered a Jack Daniels over ice and said something to the bartender. He glanced over his shoulder at Dillon and Camille then turned away again. The bartender poured himself a brandy and came around the bar.

"It must be your lucky day," he told Dillon. "This is the skipper of 'The Sea Dragon'. He's willing to take you to the mainland for the right price."

Dillon turned to Camille and said in Swedish: "Our handsome friend here wants to take us to the UK. He works for the men we're tracking and is no doubt dangerous. Should we accept his kind offer?"

"I can't think why we shouldn't – he's likely to take us straight to the man we want?" Camille replied in Swedish, being careful not to say Elliott Stark's name.

Dillon smiled, "Let's hear what he's got to say first."

"What's your name, skipper?"

"It doesn't matter what my name is and I'm not interested in yours". He bristled with arrogance and bravado.

"Oh, you're very refreshing – yet a little on the melodramatic side." Dillon said smiling.

The skipper eyed Dillon with suspicion. He was a wiry lean looking man with thick black hair cropped. But it was the scaring across his face that was most noticeable. Camille was right; a sinister looking devil. Raising his glass to thick set lips he swallowed the contents in a single gulp and crossed to the door. Paused and glanced back at Dillon, face expressionless.

"The Sea Dragon sets sail within the hour at high tide. If you want to get to England it'll cost you ten thousand pounds. Sterling."

"Ten thousand, you say. Sounds steep for a ninety-mile crossing?"

"You're the one wanting to get to England through the

back door. It doesn't matter. We leave in one hour with or without you." The skipper nodded to the bartender. "I'll be in touch with further arrangements." He spoke in Guernésiais, also known as Patois, a variety of Norman French sometimes spoken on Guernsey. Dillon sipped his pint, understanding every word spoken. The skipper turned and left.

He was on the bridge of 'The Sea Dragon' when Dillon and Camille stepped on to the deck of the hefty looking fishing trawler. They moved with care on the wet deck and around the hydraulic capstan located to the side of the opening to the hold. A young deckhand appeared out through the forward hatch wearing a bright yellow foul weather jacket and beckoned them. They had boarded the trawler at deck level. Passing through a galley and then through another internal hatch to a cabin, where there was room for only one person. Dillon heaved their holdalls onto the single bunk. A moment later the skipper started the diesel engine, they could make out shouting out on the deck as he gave the deckhand instructions.

Peering out through the tiny porthole, Dillon spotted the familiar outline of Finnegan standing on the quay. His hands deep in his jacket pockets, collar turned up to keep out the wind.

Dillon touched the butt of the Glock snug in its holster under his right arm, then leaned against the bulkhead and waited to see what happened.

* * *

Within a few minutes, they had left the harbour and were heading out into open water. The heavy rain now falling reduced visibility but Dillon caught an occasional glimpse through the porthole of the coast passing.

"Are you fitted with a tracker?" Camille asked.

Dillon pointed to his shoulder, "It's a tiny flat microchip, undetectable, imbedded just under the skin."

"Tracked by whom, GCHQ?"

"Yeah, something like that," Dillon replied, adding, "we've got company, fifty yards out."

Camille peered out of the porthole. "It's 'The Tide Runner' and by the looks of it they're shadowing us!"

'The Tide Runner' kept her distance off the starboard side of the trawler. Close enough for Dillon to see the captain, wearing the black reefer jacket his skin tone like death itself. The trawler altered course and so did the other boat as the skipper moved into deeper water to avoid running onto the rocks lurking just below the surface. Dillon frowned as he peered out of the porthole; 'The Tide Runner' had disappeared.

"I'm going up to the bridge to see if the skipper has anything to say about Finnegan."

"What should I do?"

"Stay here and lock the door. Give me five minutes and then come up to the bridge. Are you carrying?"

From its hiding place in the small of her back Camille withdrew the Beretta BU9 Nano 9mm pistol. She slipped it back in its holster and withdrew a Walther P99 AS 9mm semi-automatic pistol from its holster under her right arm.

"Good, I see you've come prepared," Dillon smiled, turned and left the cabin.

The trawler rolled on the heavy swell as she cut through the inky black water. Dillon entered the bridge from outside with the rain beating its way in behind him. The skipper turned as Dillon entered. He was at the helm; the baseball cap he'd been wearing in the pub earlier discarded exposing extraordinary black hair.

"What are you doing here? You should be in your cabin."

Dillon walked to the other side of the bridge and peered out of the windscreen.

"I have a puzzle you can help me with, skipper."

"And what puzzle might that be?" His voice laden with malevolence.

"Why we are heading south when we should on a north by north-east heading?" Dillon asked.

There was a moment of silence, except for the pounding of heavy rain on the windscreen and the squall howling straight at them.

The skipper remained seated, eyes looking straight ahead, scanning the water ahead. The move was sudden; his right hand came up gripping the .38 snubbed nose Smith & Wesson - the noise deafening in the small space of the bridge as he pulled the trigger.

Only Dillon wasn't standing there any longer. The bullet ricocheted off the bulkhead - he had dropped to the floor, rolled forward once and was now standing behind the skipper – his arm locked around his neck.

"Your mistake was thinking I'd be an easy kill." Dillon's voice remained calm and steady as he spoke the words. But the whisper from his inner psyche goaded him to kill the dark-haired scumbag, that's what Sir Hector had said – execute everyone involved. *Go on, one sharp movement of your arm and he's dead.*

Dillon hadn't heard the light-footed steps come up the companionway behind him. He wasn't sure what had just happened. Camille was screaming his name and then the lights went out. There was no pain – no pain at all. A skilful blow to the base of the neck delivered by an expert – the thought was there and yet being not there. In the same moment vision returned.

He looked up into an expressionless face, calm and yet a small muscle just under his right eye twitched involuntary at he looked at Dillon. Beneath the drift of flaxen hair pale blue eyes were empty. There was no love here, no cruelty either and he crouched beside Dillon in deliberation.

Dillon felt the sharp tip of a blade against his neck. He could see Camille being held by another man holding a gun to her throat, a look of helplessness on her face and the skipper standing beside her. Dillon played it cool for another couple of minutes. He came back to Elliott Stark, stared at him and then ran a hand across his eyes.

The Englishman hit him hard across the face. "Can you hear me, Jakob?" Dillon struggled up on one elbow and Stark smiled. "I thought I might have hit you harder than I had intended."

"It was hard enough." Dillon sat up, rubbing the nape of his neck with one hand. "Finnegan has been talking, I presume?"

"He tells me you stole a large sum of money from the safe on board 'The Tide Runner. This money belongs to the organisation. Where is it?" Stark held the Glock in his hand.

"In a safe place in Dorset – what you might call an insurance against accidental death. I counted over half a million in large denomination Euro notes. Who are you?" Dillon eyed the handgun.

"Let me introduce myself. My name is Stark, Elliott Stark.

Oh, and as you can see I relieved you of your gun."

"Finnegan and the skipper here work for you?"

"Yes, in a manner of speaking."

"In that case, the way your organisation treats its cash paying customers stinks. When I reached Dorset, Finnegan sent me ashore where I was greeted by two young inexperienced thugs who tried to rob me. When I returned to have a chat with Finnegan, I found him attempting to rape the lady over there. I don't know how well he's been doing for you but I'd say his bank account should make interesting reading."

Stark wasn't listening. He had turned to Camille, a frown on his face. He stood up and moved forward, she glanced at the floor and he put a hand under her chin and tipped it back.

"Is he telling the truth, Senora De Santi?"

Her dread had vanished. He didn't know who they were or why they'd come to Guernsey. She looked at him and nodded. Stark spun round and went back to where Dillon was still kneeling. His eyes were bleak, his expression one of utter wretchedness.

"What a world," he said. "What a filthy odious world." He took a deep breath; something clicked and he was himself again. "Please stand."

Dillon stood up, producing a six-inch stiletto blade at the same time and placed the length of the razor-sharp blade at Stark's neck. The skipper gave an angry cry but Stark waved him to silence. He stood, feet apart, fiddling with the chunky designer watch on his wrist.

"What now?"

"Now nothing," Dillon said. "I came to Guernsey to find Finnegan and finish what I'd started in Dorset. I should have shot him dead there and then."

"Why didn't you?"

"I wanted to get to the UK and fade into the countryside but Finnegan had ripped me off and then had me mugged. So, I took the money in the safe to teach him a lesson."

"Understandable enough, I suppose." Elliott Stark smiled. "I guess if you've got every law enforcement agency across Europe looking for you. Perhaps killing a man like Finnegan wouldn't bother you but you will not have the opportunity. He will. You have my word."

Dillon retracted the blade and pocketed the knife. "I see you've done your homework."

"I like to know who my clients are, Jakob."

Dillon sighed; he could feel the Armatix pistol still concealed in the small of his back, reassuring. They had frisked him but only a fashion while he was unconscious. "I've had a gutful of trouble during the past few months, Stark. Take us back to Dorset and I'll get you your money."

Stark continued to fiddle with his watch. "I don't think so. This is how it will play out, Jakob. You tell me where the money is. I will get it picked up and when I get confirmation, then I will get the skipper to take you back to the UK. But first we head for the Brittany coast. Here, you can have this back." He said handing Dillon the Glock minus the clip.

"Thanks, I need to make a call."

"Go ahead – but keep it on speakerphone."

Dillon speed dialled Rumple's number. The call was brief. "Rumple, we're on speaker and I need you to listen. You'll be getting a visit soon from one or two men who will collect that bag I left with you. Can you make sure they get it?"

"Understood. I will make sure the bag is ready for them." Rumple's voice sounded distant coming through the speaker of the phone.

"Message me when the bag has gone." Dillon broke the connection.

The skipper went back to the helm and said something in Patois to the deckhand who released Camille from his grip. Elliott Stark was still standing, feet apart and once again fiddling with the chunky designer watch on his wrist. Dillon lit a cigarette and leaned against the bulkhead.

"You know Jakob; your little stunt in Dorset has caused me significant trouble. In fact, without your particular skills being of use to my organisation you would be dead already." Stark had the look in his eyes of a flaxen haired devil, his features and good looks tainted by the severe pockmarks of teenage acne. He produced a slim silver case from his breast pocket and selected a thin black Russian cheroot, which he lit. "Tell me why you are on the Interpol most wanted list and your relationship with Miss De Santi?"

"You know why. You've read my sheet. I'm a security

hacker. Someone whom banks fear because their computer systems, no matter how state-of-the-art, have weaknesses. I find and then hack. I can rob accounts and empty them in the blink of an eye. The funds are into another account anywhere I choose. It's like stealing candy from children." Dillon smiled.

"Sounds impressive but how much did you get?" Stark asked.

"Over two years, I'd say around four hundred and fifty million Euros."

"You make it sound so ordinary."

"That's one way of putting it. But when an eagle-eyed auditor with a degree in advanced computer science spots the anomaly in corporate client accounts he launches a full-on investigation into the breach of their state-of-the-art hardware and software."

"If my information is correct Jakob – the authorities know your name but have no images of you or know in which country you live."

"Well that's simple. I can be anywhere or everywhere!" Dillon made himself sound smug. Stark looked bewildered. "The authorities, as good as they are, don't have the level of skill I have. They try to think like a criminal but never get it right. When I hack I am paranoid of being tracked by anyone. So, I let them find a trail of random IP addresses around the globe, criss-crossing through every major city. By the time they realise what they're chasing. It's too late because the heist has taken place and I've closed the back door as I left." Dillon laughed at his boast.

"They warn that you are a dangerous man who carries a gun and not to approach you. That you have association with known terrorist groups in Europe and the Middle East. No wonder they want you locked up in a cell."

"If you say so..."

"Such a vast sum of money – what has happened to it?"

Dillon didn't answer – his face taking on a stony expression.

Camille was standing on the other side of the bridge, staring out of the window, listening to the conversation between Dillon and Stark. She looked; Dillon threw her a smile.

Dillon stood within striking distance of the skipper. Just in case he tried anything untoward, watching Stark talking to

Camille – he said something, she smiled and a few moments later, laughed out loud. Stark laughed with her and that was the strangest thing. For a short time, he appeared to be a different person, which could mean he was unpredictable.

Getting to his feet. Dillon went along the companionway and out on to the main deck, breathing the sea air. The good salt air, the smell that always brought his boyhood holidays back to him, wherever he was.

Dillon's phone vibrated in his pocket. Rumple's text confirmed that the Cooper twins had collected the bag with the money in. Trackers were in the base of the bag and the handle, with micro-trackers placed on the money. London was live with the GPS signal being transmitted by the devices.

Stark received a confirmation message from Darren Cooper at the same time.

Chapter 6

Northern Coast
France

A solitary granite three storey building stood steadfast before the tall pine trees fringing the half-moon cove that was a natural harbour. Tied up alongside a wooden jetty was an old wooden sailing boat that looked like it was derelict. The strong wind blowing off-shore making the rigging moan and creak as it lifted and dropped with each rolling wave.

The current was flowing in fast. Soon the water level would rise and with it the opportunity for the 'The Sea Dragon' to get alongside the jetty without running aground in shallow water. On the beach, an older man was working on the hull of a rowing boat.

Dillon noted landmarks as the trawler passed the headland into the cove. The granite building stood alone with only the pine trees as a backdrop. They came alongside the jetty with the trawler's bow thrusters churning the water below them. Dillon leaned close and with his voice a whisper spoke to Camille.

"You understand these people have no intention of taking us to England, right? We've seen too much of their operation."

"How do you want to play this?"

"Stark believes I am the biggest liability as I have a grudge against Finnegan, which makes me dangerous to their operation. So, we go along with whatever they've got in store for us for the time being." Dillon caught a whiff of her expensive perfume. "Let me guess, Chanel?"

"Okay." She sounded sceptical. "Yes, Coco Mademoiselle. What if we're separated?"

"Stay in character. Don't give them cause to think anything else. Anyway, Stark has other ideas for you!" Dillon said matter-of-factly.

There was a moment of silence between them before Dillon drew her closer and kissed her. A long smouldering kiss filled with passion which only broke when the deckhand slammed his open palm on the cabin door.

"Hey! In there, Mr Stark wants you up on deck right away." His voice diminished over the noise of the engines.

Camille touched Dillon's lips with the tip of her finger. "I thought you would never do that, Mr Dillon." She smiled at him.

They left the intimacy of the cabin and walked out onto the deck of 'The Sea Dragon' and then along the jetty towards the granite building. Dillon looked around with interest, establishing his bearings, searching for anything that might become useful should the situation arise.

The small painted sign had the word Hotel, an arrow pointed up to the granite building. A flight of steep stone steps led up to a high wall. Stark turned through an archway and halted inside a cobbled courtyard. The place had a strangeness about it. A shutter had broken loose, swinging to and fro in the wind on the second floor. When Dillon glanced up, a curtain moved at the adjoining window, pulled to one side by someone.

Camille stood with her holdall on the cobbles in front of her. Stark picked the holdall up for her, leaned in close and murmured something to her and led the way. The reception area had been decorated and furnished with an air of calm in abundance.

Dillon followed Stark and Camille inside, the skipper stayed a few steps behind him. Inside there was calmness, the only sound coming from the loud ticking of a clock on the wall. Stark stood twiddling with and rotating the chronograph bezel of his watch. Dillon looked up at the amazing coloured glass zenith three floors above them. A sweeping ornate stone elliptical staircase caressed the walls all the way to the top floor.

Elliott Stark led them through to a large room with a polished oak bar at the far end commanding the room. The natural stone floor had multi-coloured thick pile rugs laid with a casualness amongst comfortable antique leather sofas and low back easy chairs.

Stark had gone behind the bar and was pouring a large

cognac. Looking up, he asked Dillon if he would like to join him.

Dillon accepted the drink and downed it in one gulp. Stark took a swig and placed the brandy glass down on the polished bar top. He glanced at Dillon and then towards the bar where a small worried-looking man of sixty entered through the rear door. He wore a chef's trousers, a laundered white tee-shirt and was wiping greasy fingers in a small towel tucked into his belt.

"Ah, there you are, chef Dubois. There will be two extra guests for dinner this evening." Stark said.

"Yes, Monsieur Stark."

"How many guests are staying in the hotel, Stark?" Dillon asked.

"Miss De Santi and yourself, along with three others, Jakob. This is my hotel, closed at present for the winter. I keep chef and his wife here all year round to maintain the place and keep things up together." He glared at Dillon, the devil in his eyes, furious at being questioned but keeping civility towards him. The undertone to his voice told the story, tension and irritation.

The chef's wife, Madame Dubois came through to the bar and after Stark had spoken to her she led Dillon and Camille up to their rooms.

They mounted the spiral flight of stairs to the first floor and moved along a poorly lit corridor with small colourful paintings on whitewashed walls. Madame Dubois opened the door and gestured for Dillon to enter.

The room was pleasant enough, of an average size with a single bed standing with its oak headboard against the back wall and a narrow bedside cabinet alongside it. A solitary painting hung on the wall above the bedhead. The artist had used vivid colours to illustrate the vibrancy of the autumn forest scene, which Dillon thought somewhat out-of-place hanging in a hotel by the sea.

Madame Dubois turned, was about to leave. "Chef Dubois has asked me to ask you if you have any special dietary needs, Monsieur."

Dillon shook his head, "Thank you, Madame."

"Dinner will be at seven-thirty sharp. Anything else you wish for, you must see Monsieur Stark."

"And who does Monsieur Stark report to?"

Madame Dubois frowned, looking bewildered. "I don't understand, Monsieur."

"I believe you, Madame."

Madame Dubois shrugged and went out. Dillon put his holdall on the bed, moved to the window and gazed out. So, this was Stark's safe house.

Behind him, someone said, "Hey dude, welcome to The Liberty hotel."

* * *

Down on the jetty the crew of a small fishing boat were unloading their catch to shrieking seagulls in a whirl of beating wings and snapping beaks. Down on the beach, Savage threw stones into the sea. He turned and moved back from the water's edge towards Dillon, tall, handsome, a strong angular face; dark brown cropped hair and dark brooding eyes. Sam Savage? It was a reasonable name as any. He had the shoulders of a heavyweight boxer who could go the distance and Dillon eyed him with a wariness.

He pulled his hoodie up against the wind and rain, producing a packet of cigarettes, he lit one. "So, you're from Sweden?" Savage asked.

"That's it, I am from Stockholm."

"They tell me that's quite a town."

"The best - you should try it."

The American stared at him. "You must be joking. With my rap-sheet the feds would pick me up the moment I stepped off the plane." He laughed, adding, "That's why I'm here, man."

It was a plain statement of fact, without acrimony in it and Dillon shrugged. "Yes, I know what you mean. Isn't it why we're all here? Rule breakers, the lot of us." This time it was Dillon who laughed.

The American was interested. "I've been wondering why you are using the back door into the old country with the rest of us."

"Well, like you and the lady, I travelled here because I've been a naughty boy."

Savage grinned, producing his packet of cigarettes for the second time and offered him one. "The law must want you badly."

"About forty years' worth in a high security prison - that's if I'm lucky and the judge isn't feeling harsh on the day."

Savage whistled. "Man, you must have been a bad, bad boy."

"I have a penchant for robbing banks." Dillon looked along the beach and beyond to the sea. "You're a long way from the States so you must have pissed off someone, bigtime."

"Not far enough." Savage looked anxious. Something in his voice changed, was it the accent that had slipped but Dillon remained silent?

"What are you a terrorist or something?"

"Hell dude, no. I'm not into that shit."

"Then what is it?"

"Okay, I suppose there's no harm telling you dude. I'm what I like to call a mortality technician."

"Sounds like an interesting line of work." Dillon commented. "So, what is a mortality technician?

"Hey dude, just kidding with you. I was a professional assassin for the crime syndicate."

"Was?"

"Yeah–was! Taking out a US Senator in Chicago was not a good move. The Federal authorities took the hit personally and put me on their most wanted register."

"Really, I wonder why?" Dillon grinned.

"The syndicate got me clear of the States to the Caribbean and then onto Europe by way of this crowd."

Dillon had heard enough and didn't believe a word of Savage's story. "This is about the nicest beach I've stood on since The Bahamas."

"That's what I thought three days ago–now it's just a drag. I want to get moving."

"What are your plans when you get across the Channel?"

Savage shrugged and then grinned. "Let's say that the syndicate has arranged for me to aid our UK partners in eradicating problems."

"How long will the UK play host to you? Dillon asked.

"As long as it takes–once I'm over there I'll head for London where I'll simply blend with the scenery. Even with thousands of CCTV cameras I'll still be able to move around as just another face. You just need to change your appearance regularly."

Dillon kept from laughing at this fake's bullshit but decided to press the American further. "Are there any others travelling with us?"

"Five of us in total, dude. In fact, if you look over your left shoulder you'll see two of them coming down the path from the cliff top."

The old man was of Chinese origin wearing a heavy black overcoat that gave him a strangely withered look. His tanned skin, creased with age, was drawn over the jawbones. He walked with a distinct limp on his right side and carried a black cane for support. Dillon was intrigued by the young Oriental woman walking at his side.

"His name is Chang, and he's an odd one. I mean really odd - doesn't say much and always eats alone in his room. All I know is, he's something high-up in the Triads of Macau."

"What's the story with the woman?"

"Her name is Mingyu, meaning bright Jade in Chinese. She's Chang's, well I don't know what she is–but she's Chang's something, dude."

"So, we can assume that she's a dangerous companion, then."

Mingyu was about twenty-five, with solid black hair and a skin that was translucent. She seemed cold and wore a full-length cashmere overcoat.

"Why would a senior member of the Triads be travelling like this and with nobody as guard other than Mingyu; makes me wonder about Mr Chang?"

They paused, the old man gasping for breath.

"A cold damp day Mr Chang, don't you agree?" Savage said in a loud voice.

Savage and Dillon walked up the beach to where they were standing. "This is Mr Jakob, a new arrival. He'll be travelling with us."

The old man showed no surprise. "Ah, yes, I met a lady earlier. A Miss De Santi, she spoke of you."

"You've met her?" Dillon said.

"Just before we left for our walk," Mingyu said.

Chang held out his hand which Dillon shook, surprised at

the firmness of the grip for a man of his age.

Mingyu seemed embarrassed and tugged at the old man's overcoat sleeve. "Come along, Chang Sir, we must get back to the hotel. This cold air will not agree with you. Nice to meet you Jakob, Sir."

Dillon watched them walk slowly towards the steps that led up to the hotel.

He turned and found Savage watching him intently. "You look confused?"

"Just can't make head nor tail of it, dude."

"What's that?"

"There's more to old Chang than meets the eye. He's travelling to the UK - way under the radar but why."

"And that is?"

Savage looked at Dillon for a moment before answering him. "He's on his way to the UK to surprise someone and it's not a friendly visit."

"You like assuming things, Savage?" Dillon said.

"I know the way of the Triads."

"I don't know about Triads but I do know about people." Dillon lied easily.

"Neither do I, dude." Savage grinned, and the moment passed. "You want something to eat, we'd better move or we'll miss out."

They made their way back to the hotel, passed the jetty and up the steep flight of steps. Dillon commented on a new boat, 'The Tide Runner' which was tied up alongside the trawler. Dillon pointed towards the fifty-foot motor boat. "Is that the boat?"

Savage nodded. "It fits within the scheme of things, wouldn't you say?"

"It's a scruffy weather-beaten tub with a turn of speed they say can outrun anything. Finnegan is her skipper."

"What do you make of him?"

Savage shrugged. "He's a scumbag and a drunk but he knows these waters like the back of his hand."

"What about the first mate–Le Croix?"

"Frightened of his own shadow and terrified of Finnegan. Lives on Guernsey, has done all his life."

"What's Stark's story?"

Savage smiled. "Hey dude, you like the questions, don't you?"

Dillon shrugged. "Suit yourself."

"Okay, I will. Elliott Stark is an enigma–no one gets close to that dude. Haven't you seen the devil in his eye?"

"Is he married?"

"Stark." The American laughed. "That's funny; he studied to be a priest - a Roman Catholic priest."

"And how would you know?"

"I needed a smoke. So, I knocked on Stark's door but the room was empty."

"And curiosity got the better of you?"

"Dude, what else could I do? I needed a smoke, so I let myself in and had a little snoop around his room. He must have had a thousand cigarettes stashed in a large suitcase. But something that caught my eye was a photograph of a group of men dressed in military dress suits. Who was standing right in the middle of them–yes, Mr Elliott Stark dressed in the colours of the Household Cavalry Regiment?"

Dillon wondered what had happened for Stark to lose his commission. He pictured Stark's tortured, unsmiling face, the face of a murderer he understood but the face of a high-ranking army officer... it didn't seem possible.

He was still thinking about it as they turned into the courtyard of the hotel.

Chapter 7

The main lounge bar was empty when they entered, Savage walked behind the bar and took a bottle of Jack Daniels and two glasses from the shelf.

"Join me?" he said.

Dillon nodded. "I see no reason we shouldn't."

There came a sudden holler of anger as chef Dubois appeared through the rear door. "Put those glasses back. Brash American yob."

Savage looked him over, not a flicker of emotion on his face. "Hey dude, sure I'm not deaf," he said, in reasonable French.

He unscrewed the bottle and filled both glasses. Chef Dubois took a quick step towards him, grabbed the American by the shoulder and spun him around and held a curved boning knife to his throat.

"Dubois!" Elliott Stark spoke from the doorway, his voice full of steel, countenancing no denial.

Dubois turned. "They don't even pay, monsieur," he muttered under his breath.

Stark ignored him and stepped forward. He was wearing a pair of beige chino trousers, an expensive looking white shirt and a tailored navy-blue blazer. He carried a slim leather-bound book in one hand, a finger marking his place.

"Please gentlemen, be my guests."

"Are you going to join us?" Dillon enquired.

"Thank you, I will have one with you and then I have to attend to business."

Stark came and sat at the bar; Dillon filled a shot glass and placed it on the bar. He emptied his glass in a single swallow and filled it again. Chef Dubois, scowling, took a bottle of Cognac and a glass for himself and sat at the other end of the bar alone.

"You've been for a walk, I see," Stark said.

Dillon nodded. "That's right. It's a lovely spot you have here."

"Suppose it is."

"I'm wondering when we'll be leaving here?"

"Don't know. We are waiting for another passenger. It depends when he arrives."

"Is that today, tomorrow, next week. I want to know?"

"At the right time, Jakob. No need to worry yourself. We are professionals; we know what we are doing."

Behind them a soft voice said, "May I join you?"

Camille stood in the doorway, her flawless features set off to perfection by the colourful scarf coiled around her slender neck. The gold Cartier on her wrist got Sam Savage's attention and this interested Dillon the most. Savage gave her an on-the-spot appraisal, as a connoisseur of fine wine would, challenging the vintage just before taking the first sip. The cork is drawn and enough of the bottle's contents poured into the tasting-glass, the valuable liquid glowing in the glass releasing natural aromas. Anticipation increasing until that first sip. Dubois gazed at her with ill-concealed lust. Stark looked indifferent. His pale complexion making his eyes darker and then a strange thing happened. He smiled and his face lightened.

He moved forward and gave her his arm. "Dinner awaits. Shall we go?" he said taking her through into the dining room.

He had left his leather-bound book on the bar counter and Dillon stole a quick glance. The pages contained timetables of tides and coastal charts for the British Isles with handwritten various notations by the calculations.

Dillon frowned. Stark appeared on the surface to talk as a pro but could he deliver what he promised. He wondered if he was as competent, or just relying on the likes of Finnegan and the skipper of the Sea Dragon. He emptied his glass, nodded to Savage, and they walked in to dinner.

* * *

There was a garden contained by high brick walls behind the hotel, a sad sorry excuse of a place. The vegetable patches were overrun with weeds and messy from lack of proper attention. There were flower borders, but it was too early in the year for any blooms, only weeds and brambles thrived and spilled over onto the narrow gravel paths.

Camille walked with Stark at her side. He said something, and she laughed good-humouredly. Dillon watched them from behind his room window, their voices muffled on the other side of the glass. Stark looked up. Dillon stepped back behind the curtain.

"First time I've seen him smile as if it was genuine," the American said.

"She's impressed him," Dillon replied, "but I'm not sure how."

Stark leaned in towards and murmured to Camille, turned and left her alone in the garden. She walked by herself, looking up at the herring gulls soaring overhead. A moment later, chef Dubois appeared.

He was drunk and swayed a tad as he moved forward, staring at her unswervingly. She didn't see him, still intent on the noisy gulls overhead, until he reached out and grabbed her shoulder roughly. She spun round, placing her weight on her left foot and snapping her right leg back to strike him in the ribs. He fell on to the gravel path with a heavy thud, writhing and screaming with the piercing pain in his side. Camille looked at him with genuine concern.

"Monsieur Dubois, I could have killed you." She hurried to help him up, but he caught hold of the sleeve of her rain mac, pulled her close and tried to kiss her. He got a response but not the one he wanted. Camille brought a knee up between Dubois's legs as her elbow broke his nose. She tried to get away from him but he caught hold of her ankle and laughed as he tightened his grip.

Savage beat Dillon to the door. They descended the stairs, along the passage and out through the kitchen. They were too late.

Stark stood half between them and Dubois, Camille lay on the ground a short distance away from the chef. Dillon motioned for Savage to stay still and quiet as Stark moved purposefully towards Dubois. He stood over him, looking at his bloodied face, fiddling with his watch. Dubois had genuine terror in his eyes as if he knew what was coming.

Dubois tried to get up. He scrabbled up onto his knees trying to stand up, his clothing wet and grubby, hair dishevelled from his struggle with Camille. Stark grabbed the chef from behind and with a fluid single movement drew the garrotte wire around his throat.

"If you ever mess with any of my guests again Dubois, I will kill you. Understand?"

The chef nodded. Stark tightened the wire, drawing blood as it bit into soft flesh. The flesh opened and a crimson curtain oozed onto his pristine white shirt. He released the wire that retracted back into the watch case. So that was it, Dillon pondered.

Dubois rolled over without a sound. Camille stood looking at him, a dazed look on her face. Stark moved over to her, put an arm around her shoulders and led her back into the hotel past Dillon and Savage without a glance.

Dillon turned Dubois over and dropped to one knee. He held his forefinger to the unconscious man's neck, checking for a pulse.

"Is he alive?" Savage asked.

"He's alive. Fainted dead away with fright, I expect. Stark knew what he was doing. He's marked him so he wouldn't ever forget, it's that simple. A plaster should be enough."

"Did you see his face?"

"Yes, I saw Stark's face." Dillon nodded. "It reminded me of something in Hitchcock's film, Psycho."

"This whole thing is a nightmare."

Dillon grinned. "You imagine a nightmare is this? Expect things to get far worse before we reach the UK."

The American looked at Dillon but remained silent as he reached to pick up the unconscious Dubois off the wet ground. Together they dragged him inside the chateau.

* * *

Later in the afternoon, the rain came again with suddenness, shrouding everything in a grey curtain. Madame Dubois had taken on the role of cooking along with her other chores around the hotel. She came into the lounge bar, threw logs on the open fire and left at once without a word. Dillon, Savage and Camille were at the bar when she came in. The three of them looked at each other without commenting.

Dillon finished his drink, walked to the door which led

to the dining room. Stark and Dubois sat at a table, talking in low tones, a bottle of rum between them. Otherwise the place was empty, except for Dan Lacroix, the first mate on the Tide Runner. He stood by the main entrance to the hotel gazing at the rain falling and large rolling waves crashing on to the beach. This was a good opportunity and one that Dillon might not get again. He turned, glanced back at Lacroix before moving along the passageway, pausing at a door marked Manager's Office. The lock clicked as the pick found its mark, an old mortice that opened with the first skeleton key. Dillon stepped through the open-door way.

The dimly lit room was small, ten feet by eight at most, with an old wooden desk against one wall and a map of Guernsey hanging above it. An archaic swivel chair the only other piece of furniture in the room. Otherwise, it was bare and devoid of clues of who the person was who worked here. Dillon headed straight to the desk and tried to open the first drawer at the top, locked like the others but opened with the jiggle of another skeleton key. He pulled it open to show what was inside, nothing except for a passport.

Dillon picked up the burgundy document with the official Swedish crest and flicked through the pages. He paused at the photo image, using his phone to send an image of the page to London for confirmation. A reply came at once.

Passport of the deceased
Alex Bergfalk
Swedish national

Dillon returned the passport back to the exact position he'd found it, closed the drawer and then locked it. He rummaged through the other drawers finding other passports. He shot a video clip of them. Then uploaded to Sir Hector's secure server in London. There was nothing more of interest. He checked that everything was as he had found it, opened the door and stepped out. Savage moved from the shadow of an alcove at once opposite and smiled.

"Have you been snooping, dude?" he demanded.

Dillon smiled. "My mistake - thought it was the cloakroom," he said, still not knowing if he could trust Savage.

"Man, that's the story of my life, always walking into the wrong room," the American laughed.

The sound of a car pulling up in the carpark could be clearly heard at the rear of the hotel. They moved back along the passageway and peered out of a small window. A new Range Rover parked by the rear entrance with Stark and Dubois standing beside it. Dubois opened the rear door and a young man emerged, wearing a heavy black trench coat with a baseball cap. He was Chinese, around thirty years of age and built like a bull, with a round, smooth, enigmatic face.

"Dude, this gets more the United Nations every minute," Savage whispered.

Dillon nodded, as the Range Rover drove away and Dubois picked up the new arrival's bags. "Presumably, the passenger we've been waiting for. We'd better get back to the bar and see what the form is."

In the bar Stark was making introductions and when Dillon and Savage appeared, he turned with a pleasant smile. "Ah, now we are here. Gentlemen, let me introduce you to Mr Feng."

He stepped forward to shake hands. Close up, he was in his late thirties, with a smile of exceptional charm and white teeth. "So, you are Swedish?" he said to Dillon. "I have had many dealings with firms in your country. I am from Hong Kong."

He shook hands with Savage with less enthusiasm and little or no talking. He left a moment later with Stark and Dubois, who still looked peaky. A great strip of surgical tape pasted across his throat.

"At least he shook hands," Savage observed. "They don't dig Americans, do they?"

"What makes you think that?"

"Because the Chinese think Americans brash, that's why."

"The Chinese people don't think in that way. More likely he thinks you are chippy about him," Dillon smiled. "And, before you start feeling sorry for yourself, I'm in there too."

Dillon went back to the front reception hall and put on his overcoat hanging from one of the wooden pegs. Savage came through behind him. "Going somewhere?"

"I need fresh sea air."

"Mind if I tag along dude?"

"Suit yourself."

The American pulled up the hood on the Parka coat and they out into the rain. It wasn't just rain, it was a heavy downpour - walking through a waterfall couldn't get any wetter. The drops struck the wet courtyard, pitting the surface as if they were bullets from heaven. Dillon descended the steps towards the beach, thinking about the assignment so far.

There was the organisation, simple in its aims. Who could get anyone who'd pay the high price in cash, up-front, to get them across the Channel and into the UK? Except that they will cut your throat in the right circumstances. Meeting Finnegan and Stark made that fact easier to believe by the minute.

What was Elliott Stark's story? On the surface he appeared to be an easy-going man. In reality, he was a vicious and ruthless killer, who'd go to any length to preserve his liberty. Mr Chang and Mingyu were easy enough to accept and Savage fitted into place but Mr Feng from Hong Kong? Now he was an interesting piece of the jigsaw.

He paused at the far end of the beach, gazing at the grey tumultuous sea. Savage nudged him in the ribs. "You see what I see? They're on board the Tide Runner with that dude, Feng."

Dillon squatted beside a large rock, pulling Savage beside him. Stark and Feng had left the Tide Runner and were walking along the wooden jetty towards the Sea Dragon. As he watched, they scrambled onto the deck and disappeared along the companionway.

"What are they doing?" Savage looked at Dillon from under the sodden hood.

Dillon didn't answer. He got to his feet running towards the water and walked back along the beach towards the jetty with Savage. The rain was still falling, a mist wafted in off the sea affording them a modicum of camouflage. The boat on the beach for repairs remained on its side. Dillon moved beside its hull, which gave excellent cover.

After a few moments, they moved forward again and reached the shelter of the jetty. Dillon paused.

Savage said, "What did you have in mind dude?"

"Follow me, I want to know what they're discussing."

He worked his way along the heavy timbers, climbing to the next level at the point where grey-green water slapped against the timbers. The heavy smell of the sea hung over everything, salt-water and seaweed, harsh and pungent, both unpleasant. He crouched in a cross-piece, Savage right behind him. There were footsteps on the deck above their heads.

Stark and Mr Feng were talking in Cantonese. Dillon strained every nerve to hear what was being said but could only catch odd words and phrases. There was a sudden burst of laughter and then footsteps drummed on the boards overhead as they walked away.

"What were they saying?" Savage asked.

Dillon shook his head. "I couldn't catch everything but piecing it together, Feng has travelled from a place called Hades Keep, transported by a man named Montanari. Does that make any sense to you?"

Savage nodded. "Montanari is not a name I've heard but Hades Keep I've heard the name before. I overheard a conversation between Stark and that rough-house skipper Finnegan."

Dillon scrambled back between the cross-ties and jumped onto the wet sand, Savage followed closely. They walked back along the jetty, looking at the deck of the Tide Runner. It was a depressing sight in daylight, shabby and derelict looking. The original dinghy had been swapped for a smaller craft with a more powerful outboard motor attached to the stern.

"One thing's for sure," he said, "if the Coastguard turns up, or that scrapheap goes down, we will be swimming. That thing won't hold over four people."

They walked back towards the hotel. As they moved up the steep steps, Savage laughed.

"What's so funny?" Dillon asked.

"You are funny." Savage contrived to look innocent. "You're the only Swedish national I've ever met who could speak fluent French. Have a good working knowledge of Chinese and Italian and also speak English as a Brit. Those Swedish must be something."

"Fuck off," Dillon said and moved up to the hotel courtyard.

* * *

Entering the hotel lobby, Stark stood alone at the bar whilst

Dubois was pouring himself a Cognac. The Englishman turned and smiled. "Ah, there you are. We were looking for you."

"Walking on the beach," Dillon said. "Was it important?"

"I think so. You'll both be happy to know we're leaving tonight at around nine-fifteen."

"How long will the crossing take?"

"Something around seven hours. If the weather holds, you'll be left on a beach near to Poole on the Dorset coast."

"Will there be a welcoming committee like last time?"

"No Jakob. That was unfortunate and as I've said I am very sorry it happened. You will be met by my people on the other side. We should be able to put you ashore around four-thirty tomorrow morning. They will have transport and get you to London by seven-thirty where we leave you to fend for yourself."

"What if the Coastguard turns up?" Savage asked.

"What of it? You'll be on your own."

"How do you figure on getting past them without being stopped, dude?"

"Oh, I see what you mean. The Coastguard and border agency will pose no problem," Stark laughed.

"How can you be so sure, Stark?"

Stark looked at the American, surprised. "Because, Mr Savage, I can be and it never does, I can assure you. I'll see you both later."

He went out, closing the door behind him.

Dillon was wondering what Camille was up to and Savage sighed. "He's one arrogant self-assured asshole. You think he's telling the truth that nothing ever goes wrong?"

"Do you?" Dillon said.

Savage wandered over to the window without answering. He stood staring out of the window, before turning around and looking back at Dillon.

Savage broke first, his face creasing into a smile. "I know one thing dude. This evening has been an interesting one."

Chapter 8

Except for the gentle lapping of water against the jetty's timbers, an eerie silence surrounded the jetty.

A disturbing place in daylight, let alone at night, with only a single spotlight illuminating the Tide Runner.

In the harsh light, the vessel looked less attractive than ever. Peeling paint and years of neglect had taken its toll, or, perhaps that's how it was meant to look.

Dan Lacroix moved around on deck checking that everything had been secured down properly when the party from the hotel arrived. Stark led the way, carrying Camille's holdall. She thought his gesture was nothing more than solicitude, helping her down the companionway. The others followed; Dillon and Savage helped old Mr Chang on-board, Mingyu and Feng stayed close.

Stark called Dillon back, grabbing his sleeve. "A quiet word before you go below, Jakob."

"Is there a problem?" Dillon enquired politely.

"Your gun," Stark held out his hand. "You won't need it while you're aboard."

Dillon shrugged, produced the Glock and handed it over to him. "I trust you will give it back?"

"Naturally, once we arrive at our destination. Now let's join the others inside." He looked up and nodded to Finnegan who stood at the wheel behind the windscreen. A moment later the engines started and Lacroix cast off the forward and stern lines.

Dillon descended the companionway to the day cabin. The others were all seated on either side of a central table. They looked farcically formal as if they were attending a wake where the body was nowhere to be found. Savage pushed up to make room for him on the padded bench and smiled.

"What kept you dude?"

Before Dillon could answer Stark appeared. He leaned on the end of the table, his hands taking his weight. "Ladies and gentlemen, we are starting the most dangerous leg of our journey. I must insist that you stay here in the cabin for your own safety. If the weather holds and the forecast is favourable you will be back on land in around seven hours from now at a secluded cove near a small village near to Poole on the Dorset coast."

"Once ashore our people will be there to meet you. Each of you will receive a one-way ticket to the place of your choice and a brand-new passport. You'll then be taken to the nearest train station nine miles away in a town called Wareham. The line runs straight through to London Waterloo. After that you're on your own. Are there questions?" No one spoke and he smiled. "You'll find sandwiches and coffee in the galley if anyone feels hungry. I'll see you later."

He left them as the Tide Runner moved away from the jetty. Dillon peered out of the nearest porthole and saw Dan Lacroix standing on the jetty under the light as they moved out to sea. He walked away and Dillon sat again.

Savage offered him a cigarette. "Well, what do you think now?"

"Stark talk as if he knows what he's doing, so far." Dillon leaned across to Camille. "Okay?"

She smiled brightly, "I'm fine, just fine. Elliott has been very kind. He gives off such confidence, don't you think?" Camille gave Dillon a look of warmth as she spoke the words loud enough for the others to hear.

"Let's hope he is as proficient as he is confident or is it arrogance!" Dillon smiled.

Dillon leaned back. Thinking about the incident with the Glock would make him mindful of Elliott Stark in the future. Stark having taken it from him meant that he felt nervous that Dillon carried a weapon. The motive was certainly sinister and Stark was taking every precaution to reduce the risk of anyone shooting at him should there be any trouble. Not that it mattered for Dillon who had long ago learned by bitter experience never to leave anything to chance. Still he had his Armatix Ip1 semi-automatic pistol strapped to his right leg just above the ankle with a piece of surgical tape.

He sat back, eyes half closed and watched Mr Chang who studied a book at the far end of the table next to Mingyu. Dillon wondered what it contained and in the same moment thought how Stark spoke near perfect Chinese. Yes, the more he pondered this, the more interesting his association with Chang and Feng became.

Dillon knew it would be a rough passage to the UK but so far, the sea felt placid for the time of year. He had been around boats most of his life and knew the waters around northern France and the Channel Islands. Because of this, he simply kept track of their progress by the speed at which the boat travelled and marker lights along the way.

Pots and pans, along with everything else that wasn't secured, crashed onto the floor as the boat pitched deeply in the turbulent water. The high tide rushed in around the Channel Islands which raised the level of water by as much as forty feet. Mr Chang was suffering from sea-sickness in spite of the pills which Stark had given to him at the hotel just before leaving. The old man didn't look well.

It wasn't just the pitching and rolling of the Tide Runner which caused his nausea. But also, the strong stench of diesel coming up from the engine room below that had progressively got worse by the hour. Dillon peered through the porthole as they passed La Corbière Lighthouse on the extreme south-western point of Jersey.

He told Camille, "It'll get much worse than this as we pass through an area called The Minquiers."

"What are these Minquiers?" Camille asked, bewildered.

"They're a group of islands and rocks just off of the Channel Islands that can be tremendously dangerous at night time. The currents running through this stretch of water is treacherous and the channels narrow between the rocks. If the weather holds we have a chance. If it blows up, we should take a big breath and hope that the Irishman at the helm knows his way around these waters."

Savage made a wry face, "Hey dude, much more of this diesel stench and I'll be throwing-up."

Dillon's voice lowered, "I'm not happy with it. I'm going up top and have a word with our friend."

The door of the companionway had been locked from the

other side. Dillon hammered on it with his clenched fist. After a while, it opened and Stark peered at him.

"What do you want, Jakob?"

"We're getting an overwhelming stench of diesel below," Dillon told him. "Mr Chang has vomited and isn't looking good."

Stark crouched and sniffed. A frown appeared on his face. "I see what you mean. Better bring him up for a breath of fresh air while I get Finnegan to check the engine."

Between them, Savage and Dillon took the old man up the companionway with Mingyu following right behind them. Once outside, the old Chinese man recovered his composure and colour had returned to his face. The easy rolling swell of the sea with the light wind blowing, created a calmness. Dillon was right this old tub was a wolf in sheep's clothing. Finnegan crouched beside the hatch on deck, which gave access to the engine bay. He disappeared from view; Dillon left Savage to stand by Chang and Mingyu and then crossed the deck to the open hatch.

The engine bay only had four feet of headroom. Finnegan had to squat at the bottom of the short ladder while he fumbled for the light switch. He found it and the next moment the lights came on and the problem obvious. An inch of diesel slopping around his boots.

He edged forward and disappeared from sight, reappearing a moment later. "Serious, is it?" Dillon asked, as the Irishman came up the ladder.

Finnegan ignored him, replaced the hatch and strode off up to the wheelhouse. Dillon returned to Savage, who now leaned on the rail with the others.

"What's up dude?" Savage demanded.

Dillon shrugged. "Finnegan wasn't forthcoming. But I'd say there's a leak in the fuel line."

"That's correct." Stark joined them, a match flaring in his cupped hands. "As it happens, we have two engines but can run easily on one of course. Finnegan has now cut the fuel to the faulty line, so things should improve greatly now."

"We'd like to stay up on deck for a while," Dillon said, "if only for ten minutes until the stench of fuel clears."

"That's not going to happen. The old man can remain with his aide but you and Savage go below and stay out of sight.

No arguments now!"

He returned to the wheelhouse as Dillon and Savage went back to the cabin. At the top of the companion the smell of diesel still lingered but nowhere as strong as it had been earlier. Camille looked queasy still sitting at the table, Feng leaned back in his seat, eyes closed, hands folded across his chest.

Dillon glanced out spotting the green and red navigation lights of a container ship out in the main shipping lane half a mile off the starboard side. He watched for a few minutes until it disappeared as if a curtain had dropped into place. He looked round to find Savage staring at him.

"It's not looking good out there. There's mist gathering off the water and that fine rain has started up again." Dillon said, hiding his annoyance of the American who had started to irritate him. He tried to send a text message to London, but the signal was down, or a GPS blocker located somewhere on board the boat was being used.

Three hours later, the sound of metal seizing, followed by a muffled explosion, pitched the boat violently. Mr Chang, Feng and Mingyu were thrown form their seats onto the floor. Dillon managed to keep his balance as had Camille and Savage. Dillon helped Mr Chang to his feet, the fifty-six-foot Tide Runner came to a dead halt, at once beginning to drift.

* * *

Dillon tried the companionway door, locked; he pounded on it with the flat of his hand. It opened at once and Stark peered in, a 9mm mini Uzi machine pistol in his hand. His face had turned very pale, the blue eyes expressionless and yet the gun didn't waver in the slightest.

"What's the problem, Stark?" Dillon asked.

"Nothing we can't handle, Jakob. Now, stay here and please keep calm." Stark replied in his best public-school drawl.

"What is this bullshit? We have a right to know what's going on." Savage snapped.

"When I'm good and ready, you'll know. Until then you stay here." Stark took one step closer to Savage and pushed the muzzle of the Uzi in the American's stomach. "It's for your own safety."

Savage looked at the Uzi and then up at Stark.

"There's no need to be aggressive."

Stark pushed Savage back, turned and left the cabin, slamming the door and locking it.

In the stress of the moment Savage's accent slipped, a surprising transformation from Californian surfer dude to the expression of a Harvard law graduate.

Old Chang had come back to life finding his feet and pacing the cabin. Feng's reaction was the most interesting. No panic, no dramatics. He sat at the table, face expressionless, eyes watchful.

Dillon unscrewed one of the portholes and peered out. The acrid smell of burning diesel filled the air and Stark and Finnegan arguing just above his head could be heard.

"It's completely knackered, I tell you," Finnegan's word came fast, his Irish accent becoming more pronounced, each word heavily laden with panic. "This old rust bucket has had its day."

"How far from the coast are we?" Stark demanded.

"The GPS registered our position just before the boat's power failed, we're less than three miles off the coast of Dorset."

"Good–we'll radio the Sea Dragon and get the skipper to come up from Guernsey to tow the Tide Runner back to France."

"No power, no radio!" Finnegan said bluntly.

"The radio has no backup power?" Stark's voice incredulous.

"Oh, it should have a backup power supply but we use mobile phones these days." Finnegan laughed. "Don't worry, this old crate isn't being towed anywhere. She's worth a lot more on the bottom of this sea for insurance. She's had her day, she should be scuttled Mr Stark."

"Well you'd better see to it then, Mr Finnegan," Stark shouted. "We'll make the rest of the journey in the inflatable. Have it made ready to sail in fifteen minutes."

The rest of the conversation got carried away on the wind and Dillon turned to face Savage, kneeling on the seat beside him.

"What's going on dude?"

"From what they're saying, it's the Tide Runner's demise. They're talking about scuttling her. Stark will take us in the inflatable the rest of the way to Poole Harbour."

"Can it be done?"

"I don't see why not. It's less than three miles to the coast and they've got a good outboard motor on that thing. Of course, there's only room for four people but I shouldn't think that will present much of a problem. Not to Stark, anyway."

The door to the companionway flung open with startling suddenness and Stark appeared, the Uzi in his hand. He waved it at Dillon and Savage.

"You two, sit and stay," Stark's voice had menace.

They both did as instructed. Dillon groped for the Armatix Ip1 pistol strapped to his leg just above the ankle.

Stark nodded at Camille. "Miss De-Santi, please go up onto the deck."

She shook her head, complete bewilderment on her face.

"But I don't understand."

Something inside Stark's head snapped. The mask of calmness cracked into a million pieces; he grabbed her roughly by the arm and bawled wildly, "You want to die, do you?" He shoved her up the companionway. "Go on – get on deck."

Mr Chang sagged into his seat as Camille stumbled out of sight and Dillon said, "What do we do Stark? Go under with the ship?"

Stark ignored him and spoke to Chang, Feng and Mingyu in rapid Chinese. "Get on deck fast. The boat is going to sink."

The Chinese departed first and Dillon remained seated with Savage, his hand fastening around the butt of the Armatix.

"I've got to give it to you, Stark. It must have taken nerve to see Alek Bergfalk off the way you did but even better, what could be better than a natural drowning..."

Stark turned and fired, blindly in a reflex action, the bullets splintering the bulkhead behind Dillon to the left of him. Mingyu screamed, Dillon sent Savage to the floor with a shove in the shoulder and brought the Armatix up fast. The bullet caught Feng on the side of the face, gouging a bloody furrow across his left cheek, splitting wood out of the doorpost.

Feng didn't utter a sound. He spun round and hurled himself up the companionway and Stark fired off another four rounds wildly. Dillon dived for cover. As the echoes died away, the door slammed shut, and the bolt clunked into place.

He got to his feet and found Savage making his way to

the companionway. Dillon got to him just in time and dragged him onto the deck, rugby style, onto the floor as a multi burst of rounds from the Uzi smashed through the door.

"Wait, Sam–wait! Don't you get it? He's expecting one of us to do that."

They both flattened themselves against the wall on the other side of the cabin. Savage said in a whisper, "You know how to handle yourself, I'll say that for you."

Dillon grinned. "You don't do too badly yourself for a Swedish spook."

Savage showed no surprise. "You know who I am?"

"Sam Savage–real name, Erik Klasson. Aged thirty-one, graduated university of Stockholm with an honours degree in criminology; recruited while still there and have been with Swedish Intelligence for three years. You're an outstanding linguist and accomplished sniper. Alex Bergfalk had been running from the authorities and you're the one who was pursuing him–until he got himself murdered aboard this boat."

"Very impressive, London has briefed you well Mr Dillon. Of course, your reputation precedes you. And please forgive my American twang; I must say that it's not as good as your Swedish accent. You had me fooled for a while but then I had the text from Sweden informing me who you are."

Dillon held out his hand. "Well, it's good to meet you Erik and a pleasure to be working alongside you."

"What now?"

"Our friends up top put Bergfalk over the side after Stark had garrotted him."

Erik Klasson straightened and moved away from the wall, his face sagging. At the same moment, the outboard motor sparked into life.

"Let's go," Dillon said and jumped into the companionway.

He fired three times, splintering the wood around the locking bolt, raised his right foot and stamped hard.

The door burst open, and he followed the steps to the deck, crouching. Too late. The sound of the outboard already fading into the mist.

Chapter 9

"What a little gem Stark is," Erik Klasson whispered. "What do we do now?"

The Tide Runner was already lying low in the water at the stern and the boat rocked with the force of the explosion.

"That bastard Finnegan must have set an explosive charge when he was in the engine bay earlier." Dillon shouted over the noise.

Water rushed through the rupture in the side of the hull below the water-mark. The fifty-six-boat was in the throes of sinking.

"Finnegan left the hatches open for good measure. They want us to go to the bottom with her." Erik Klasson shouted as he tried to steady himself against the side rail.

The Tide Runner was taking on water fast, within minutes she was floundering, becoming unpredictable as the swell undulated across the sea.

There was a sudden cry from the wheelhouse and when Dillon entered, Chang was attempting to get to his feet. He moved straight to where he lay and helped him. Yellow-tinted light made him look ancient and frail, blood covering his face from where Stark had hit him. But when he spoke, he didn't look afraid in the slightest.

"They have gone. Stark has taken the women, and that scum Feng was with them. They have left us here to drown."

Dillon supported Chang's weight, getting him out on to the deck. "Erik, go find life jackets that might still be on-board and any extra clothing for extra warmth and protection."

Klasson searched the boat and a few moments later came back with three life jackets along with three foul weather coats.

"These were all Stark left on board."

"What did you get?"

"Foul weather coats and life vests."

"Zip the coats up tight, the water will be freezing. The extra layer will at least give thermal insulation" he spoke to Chang as he helped him on with the coat and life jacket. The old man pushed his arms through the straps while Dillon scavenged for whatever could support a man's weight in the water. He moved towards the bow, he leaned over the rail spotting the cylindrical fenders that protected the side of the hull when going alongside a quayside. There were two hanging on lines below the side rail. He hauled one of them back up on to the deck, cut the lines and dragged it back to where Chang and Klasson were waiting.

"Secure the end of this line to Mr Chang's belt," Dillon told Klasson. "Better hurry we have little time."

Klasson secured the end of the fender's line to Chang's belt, instructing him to hang on to it as he jumped over the side. Understanding, he nodded and moved to the side rail.

Moaning and hissing the fifty-six-foot Tide Runner leaned over as the sea rushed in through the breach in her metal hull. The noise was disturbing and then it was silent, with rain falling and mist swirling around the doomed vessel.

They stood by the rail together, ready to go. Chang held tight to the iron railing, his knuckles white. The sea was coming over the stern pouring in across the deck in a heavy grey curtain. The boat pitched and rolled, thrashing in the waters of the choppy and wallowing sea.

Dillon glanced at his watch and then at his phone. "No signal. We're on our own from here." He placed the phone back into his jacket pocket.

Erik Klasson did the same. He looked at his phone, then back at Dillon with resignation. "Mine too."

"We're three miles off the coast of Dorset, less, the tide is due to turn soon and we'll go with it. Don't swim or you'll exhaust yourself and lose body heat. And whatever you do, don't take off any clothes that's the worst thing you could do, Mr Chang. The fender will keep you afloat. Just keep hold, go with the current and let it do the hard work. We'll try to stay together but if separated just do as I've said. Questions?"

Chang shook his head as did Klasson.

The Tide Runner gave a sudden lurch to one side and Klasson lost his balance and fell over the side rail into the freezing water. He surfaced, grabbing the rail coughing and gasping for air.

"Jesus! The water is freezing. If you don't jump now you'll be going to the bottom with this tub!"

Dillon spoke to Chang before they both launched themselves into the water. The brine hissed and foamed, lashing their faces, burning their eyes.

The old man hung onto the cylindrical fender, kicking his legs as Dillon had instructed. He had to get as far away from the sinking boat to avoid being dragged with it to the bottom.

The boat rose with the swell, inclining upwards to its destruction. Propelled up onto the lip and hovered there, a flyspeck on the cobwebbed lines of the wave. Time suspended as the whirlpool gaped under it with dire-white jaws. The boat plummeted into the black depths of the English Channel, swallowed whole in a final terrible groaning of metal.

* * *

It was the diminishing light that became the enemy, not the bitter weather, which was cruel enough. But after a while body temperature adapted itself and the fact they were wearing layers of clothing helped.

But the blackness of night was coming; even with the buoyancy of the fender Chang was struggling as he tried to keep himself afloat. He cried out for help and Dillon swam through the tumult of waves to help him. Salt spray stinging his eyes resembling hot pokers. He supported Chang from going under until Erik Klasson got to where Dillon was treading water a moment later. Between them they towed the old man on towards the coast through the barren water.

"Look over there!" Dillon pointed to the lights on the distant shore now visible as they ascended high on the swell. Klasson trod water, looking towards the coast.

"Is that Poole?"

"Depends on the tide, could be anywhere between Weymouth and Bournemouth. I'd say we're a mile off shore and lucky for us the tide is running in fast."

They swam on towards the shoreline with the help of the ingoing tide. Dillon noticed the shortening gaps between each white-capped wave.

He turned to Chang, who still hung onto the fender for life. The old man was looking pale; his skin withered stressing his bony features.

"Are you okay? Can you keep afloat?" Dillon shouted.

Chang nodded without replying. Dillon pulled him along without another word, with each stroke the burning pain in his muscles increased.

Erik Klasson kept up with Dillon, the tide carrying them inshore without delay but things would get rough.

Klasson opened his mouth in a soundless cry. Dillon turned and saw a grey-green wall of water coming in fast, blocking out the sky. There was nothing they could do. Chang, didn't even scream.

Dillon dived under, surfacing in a maelstrom of white foaming water. He struggled for breath but thanks to the life jacket remained buoyant. Chang had drifted and was now twenty or thirty feet away. Klasson thrashed around in the tempestuous water, confused and struggling to get his coordination together.

They were mid channel where the tides converged and the waters became unpredictable and treacherous.

The old man floated on his back, the fender once again having saved him from drowning. He had gone under from the immense pressure of the freak wave, only surfacing thanks to its buoyancy. He laid back, exhausted.

Dillon swam to Klasson and Chang, yelling that land was only half a mile away. He stayed in front of the other two men, strokes steady as he fought the water, lacerating salt spray stinging his weather-beaten face similar to ice burn. The sea throbbed grey with woe.

Deep inside his head, his inner demon taunted him, whispering to him from deep within his psyche. Dillon did his best to ignore the whisperings. *You're tired, frozen to your bones and exhausted, how easy it would be to finish it. Who'd miss you anyhow? Go on, Dillon, face it you've used up all your strength and then some. Give in to your need for sleep. One dip of the head into the old briny, a deep breath and that'll be it. You'll be at peace with yourself. Forever.*

"Yeah, I'm far from ready to go, pal!" Dillon said aloud.

Dillon looked back to see Klasson and Chang fifteen metres behind him making steady progress. The tide taking them along towards the shore, now a quarter of a mile away.

Finnegan had been over-cautious in his estimate of the Tide Runner's distance from the shore. Either that or they had come in faster than he had realised. He turned towards Klasson, who was still swimming with Chang in tow just behind him. He raised his arm waving until Klasson noticed, then pointed towards the shore.

"Only a quarter of a mile now!" Dillon saw Klasson raise his arm to signify that he understood and continued to swim on in the darkness.

"Not much longer now. Land is not far away." Klasson shouted to Chang.

Chang smiled but could not speak. Klasson got a bottle of water out of his pocket and opened the top with his teeth.

"Here, drink this."

He forced the old man's mouth open and poured. Chang coughed, half choked and pulled his head away. He spoke with severity, swearing he'd see Stark and Finnegan murdered for doing this to him.

Klasson grinned. "You'll have to get in line for that privilege," he said and took a swig of bottled water.

The old man's only reaction was, "If I live, I will owe you a great debt and if I should not make it, then I will rest knowing you will avenge my murderers."

* * *

Another twenty minutes and Dillon still kept a steady stroke going. He was now with Chang. Klasson had been towing the old man and felt frazzled, so Dillon grabbed hold the line. Chang floated beside him. Klasson drifted off and was out of sight for what seemed like an eternity.

Chang was still, eyes closed, his face a death mask, blue from the coldness. Dillon slapped him twice and the unseeing eyes opened. Recognition dawned. The lips moved the words only a whisper.

"Lei, Lei, is that you, my son?" he asked in Cantonese.

"Yes, my father." It took everything Dillon had to make the correct reply. "Not long now. Soon we will rest and feel the warmth."

The old man smiled, his eyes closed and with an unexpected

suddenness a wave lifted them high onto its crest. Seizing them long enough for Dillon to see cliffs through the darkness, only fifty feet away. The waves rolled in one after another the nearer they got to the beach. The noise deafening as they tumbled in towards the shore with white water crashing in a maelstrom of foam and spray on the shingle. And then moments later they were back in deeper water.

From that moment everything happened fast, helpless in the grip of the rip - tide current that dragged them with it. Dillon gripped the old man as water broke over them and another great wall of water, dark and heavy, crashed onto them. He felt a fever in his eyes.

Dillon got sent deep, too deep and found himself alone, fighting to get back to the surface. He fought to keep a grip on Chang but he got swept away from him by the strong undercurrent and back out in to deeper water. But he felt no panic for him. If it was his time, he'd die fighting.

Our instinct to survive is so primitive and so powerful that when threatened our only thought is self-preservation. Dillon's thought as he rolled over and over and then he broke surface, sucked air into his burning lungs and then went under again. The life jacket had done its job but what was now making things worse was the overcoat. He ripped them off and then his jacket as he came to the surface again.

By getting rid of the heavy clothing he became more buoyant, finding it much easier to swim as he fought to get ashore. His will to live giving him strength. Drawn from the hidden reserve that lies dormant in every human being.

His foot kicked sand, and he went under again. A rolling wave knocked him forward across large smooth rounded boulders streaming with water and he found himself up to his waist in kelp.

A surging white-capped wave roared in and careened Dillon off his feet, smashing over his fatigued body. He grabbed hold of a small rock as the raging waters washed over him. As they receded, he staggered to his feet and stumbled across the rocks to the safety of a strip of sand at the base of the cliffs.

He lay face on the sand, gasping for air for what he thought was minutes but was only a few seconds before he hauled himself to his feet. Chang, he had to find Chang. With sand in his ears and the taste of the sea in his mouth, the sound of the crashing waves still sang inside his head. Turning he picked his way through the rocks to the main beach.

He saw Chang at once through blurred vision, eyes stinging. The old man was forty or fifty feet away, lying in the shallows, the water breaking over him. Dillon ran.

A stupid gesture, running. He would be dead. He dragged the body from the water. As if by a miracle, the old eyes opened as he turned Chang over.

Chang smiled, fatigue and pain washed from his face. "Thank you."

"You're welcome, Chang sir."

Dillon held the old man's head, kneeling beside him. A moment later Chang closed his eyes as life left him.

Saddened by the old man's demise. Dillon lowered his head back onto the wet sand. He remained kneeling, eyes closed for a moment, Erik Klasson was waiting a short way along the beach watching him.

"You okay?" Dillon asked.

"I'm beaten black and blue but otherwise no permanent damage." Klasson said. "It's such a shame after the struggle Chang had to get ashore."

"Yes, a shame. But he was right you know; his murderers will be sorted."

Dillon had removed the heavy coat and had discarded the lifejacket, there was a cut along his right cheek, another on his upper arm.

"Okay, let's get out of here." Dillon said after a moment.

"Wait! Aren't we going to move him?"

"How can I put this without sounding a callous bastard?" Dillon said. "The way things are going, it'd be sensible if we didn't hang around. I don't want to be here with a dead body at my feet should anyone come along the beach. If we take him higher up the beach, Stark's people will know we must be alive and that we moved him up there. Be sure of one thing Erik, Stark will come looking for us!"

Klasson looked bewildered, "So what the hell are we going to do?"

Dillon glanced at his watch. "It's five-fifteen; it'll be daylight in fifteen minutes. We've got to get off this beach and find a phone. I'll put a call into London and give my people an update of our location. Mr Rumple will then come and get us but in the meantime, we have find somewhere quiet and off the beaten track to wait. Once we're back in Sandbanks, there will be dry clothes waiting. Luckily for you we're the about the same size and height."

Erik Klasson shook his head. "Well, whatever else you are - you are most definitely not the police."

Dillon smiled. "Now let's get off this beach, I'm freezing, tired and soaking wet through to my bones." He turned and moved off towards the cliffs through the grey morning.

Chapter 10

Sandbanks
Poole
Dorset

Montanari, Renzo Montanari." Sir Hector Blackwood turned from the window, "One of the wealthiest men in Europe, though few people have ever heard of him. He doesn't have his picture taken, but we found one which you'll find in his file. He's the billionaire businessman who's come from an era long passed. A shadowy figure who has in his past had his finger in so many pies you lose count."

"And Hades Keep?" Dillon asked. "What's that?"

Sir Hector shook his head. "Doesn't mean a thing, Montanari owns large properties in Switzerland, France, Germany and Italy. The latter is a masterpiece of architecture, a somewhat splendid palazzo in Venice on the Grand Canal. He's dropped off the radar during the past two years." He shook his head. "This makes little sense. Why on earth would a man of Montanari's wealth be involved in this?"

There was a knock at the door and Phoebe Young, Sir Hector's personal assistant, opened the door to Dillon's study and entered. She handed Sir Hector an iPad-pro. "London has just got more material from the CIA's Shanghai station."

She left the room and Sir Hector loaded the file, the content at once came up on the large wall-monitor. Each profile had an image pinned to it. "Look and see if any of these strikes a chord, Dillon?"

Chang was image number three, only his name was Chen Chi-li, and he was a high-ranking official in the Macau crime syndicate. Dillon dragged the image to the side of the screen.

"That's the man who died on the beach. He was using the

name, Chang."

Sir Hector nodded a slight frown on his face. "Chen Chi-li represented the old way of the crime syndicate. The violent way - that required those involved to do whatever to achieve their ultimate goals. He was one of the most revered and feared men in the organisation. Why he would travel in such a manner with Elliott Stark is a mystery."

The telephone buzzed; Dillon answered it and at once handed the receiver to Sir Hector. He listened for just over a minute and then looking thoughtful hung up.

"That was Hamilton calling from Swanage. He's a junior MI5 field officer whom I sent to scout out the place. We intercepted emails between Stark and a boat yard just outside the town owned by a man named Cooper."

"Cooper, you say. Does he own any other boat yards?" Dillon interjected.

"Yes, he does. His name is on the lease of a boat yard in a place called Hamworthy, near to here. He's gone missing. Last seen moving out to sea at five this morning. He was in a thirty-six-foot motor launch he uses to ferry clients out to their boats in and around the harbour."

Dillon looked at his watch and saw it was eleven fifty-five. "They'll be almost there by now, if the weather holds."

"Do you suppose he's heading for Guernsey?" Sir Hector ventured.

"Maybe, but I'm more inclined to reason he will aim for the Brittany coast."

Sir Hector nodded. "Where? Stark's hotel it's obvious, isn't it?"

"No. I reckon Stark might have run to ground at Hades Keep, wherever that might be, because I can't find any reference to it in the Brittany region."

There was a knock at the door and Erik Klasson appeared.

"Sir Hector. Let me introduce Erik Klasson of Swedish intelligence."

Sir Hector nodded at the Scandinavian intelligence officer, shook hands and lost no time in bringing Klasson up to speed.

"Forgive me for saying but you might interpret this too literally. If we look at the two words separately we find it's more likely to be a clue to a place within a place. In Greek mythology

Hades was the God of the underworld. The word Keep relates to a fortified tower built within castles by European nobility during the Middle Ages."

"Interesting, how does this help us, precisely?" Sir Hector asked, sitting in one of the antique brown leather cigar shaped club chairs.

"It means that we're looking for a castle!" Klasson replied matter-of-factly.

Dillon was looking at the map of Brittany on the screen when Phoebe Young came into the room.

"Gentlemen, Miss Young has the family information on Elliott Stark that you might find enlightening."

Phoebe Young opened the file she was holding and took a deep breath. "Elliott Stark, according to his medical records is categorised as a high functioning sociopath. Who from an early age exhibited a total lack of empathy and little understanding of social norms. These reports date back to when Stark was first evaluated, age six. Since then there have been many psychiatrists' reports up to the age of eighteen. After that he disappeared off the radar. The reports offer the same clinical conclusion that Stark ignores rules and laws of society and has a total lack of conscience. He is highly intelligent, charming and extremely good at integrating himself within many levels of society when it suits him. In truth, he is an emotionless and a manipulative personality that is callous and extremely calculating. He has grandiose self-image perceptions of himself. That is part of the charade that serves to feed his narcissism. He will stop at nothing to get what he wants and is irreverent to the consequences and punishment. Our researchers found very little personal information on Stark but we do see that he had the best education money could buy. He was sent to three public schools. He was expelled from two of them for being disruptive and verbally aggressive towards the teaching staff. At eighteen Stark attended Cambridge and graduated with a double first in mathematics. He spent a further two years at the university of Rome and then back-packed around Asia. Whilst there, he was arrested and detained by the authorities in Beijing. According to intelligence reports the Chinese held him for around seven months on spying charges but released him after the British government protested at the highest level."

"What reason did the embassy give?" Dillon asked while he studied the wall-monitor for castle locations in Brittany.

"Difficult to extract any information from the Foreign Office, they didn't fall over themselves to discuss this but I've pulled in a favour. I've been given the number of a man who was held by the Chinese at the same time and in the same place as Stark. He's an American who is here in Poole for a few days giving a series of lectures at the university and so is somewhat convenient."

Dillon glanced at the card Sir Hector passed to him. Brandon Klein, Head of research at Global Pharmaceuticals PLC, which turned out to be a shell company for the CIA. Dillon pondered. "Is there any possibility that Elliott Stark could be working for the Chinese?"

Sir Hector shrugged. "Everything is possible in this chaotic world we find ourselves in today. If he is, they certainly did a good job on him. Of course, the question is why? Why work for a communist regime? There's nothing in his file to show that he has any leaning toward communism."

"What's the story with this Brandon Klein—what's his thing?" Erik Klasson asked Sir Hector.

"Mr Klein is the chief research chemist at Global Pharmaceuticals PLC. He was giving lectures at the university of Beijing when he was arrested and held on the premise that was spying for the Americans. You go and see Mr Klein and see what you can get out of him. You will find him at the university."

"By the way, has there been any comms from Camille De Rosa?" Dillon asked.

"No, agent De Rosa has not been in touch with her control in Rome. They have informed me that the GPS signal from her phone stopped this time yesterday."

"It's most likely that the phones battery died or someone removed it," Klasson offered.

"I agree, Stark is street wise, he'd know that Camille's phone is tracked," Dillon added.

Sir Hector got to his feet. "I'll be in touch later this afternoon when I'm back in London." He was halfway to the door when the internal house phone buzzed. Dillon picked it up and called him back. Sir Hector grabbed the receiver and put it back again a second later. "Miss Young has just received a call on her mobile phone from London. A report has been picked up from the RNLI station at Portland. They pulled the naked body of a woman out of the sea off Sidmouth three hours ago. She'd been in the water for around eight or nine hours but no identification has been made as yet."

"Miss De Rosa, do you think?" Dillon asked gravely.

"Could be, or just a coincidence. Stark has a penchant for garrotting his victims before throwing them overboard. There was no mention of any neck injuries. So, we'll just have to wait until the autopsy, won't we?"

Dillon left the room quietly, murderous thoughts cascading through his mind.

* * *

Dillon drove the Porsche Panamera onto the university campus. Erik Klasson was with him as they negotiated students moving frenetically on the pavements and the roads.

"So, what's the plan now?"

"We go and find Mr Brandon Klein who is most likely giving one of his lectures," Dillon replied before getting out the luxury German sports touring car.

They walked across the carpark to the main entrance. Inside they found noise and a throng of what were freshman students being given a tour of the facilities. Dillon set off to the reception desk and was greeted by a receptionist wearing a bright fuchsia pink blouse. She looked up at him, her manner was officious but after cajoling her for a moment, she told them which lecture theatre Klein was working in.

They entered the lecture theatre through a side door. Klein was nearing the end of his talk to a near capacity audience who were evidently captivated by the American's every word. Dillon noticed the indefinable movement of Klein's eyes in their direction.

Dillon and Klasson moved towards the front of the room and introduced themselves to Klein.

"So, how can I help you gentlemen?"

His eyes were those of a man who had been through the mill a few times and trusted no one, without exception. A ragged scar ran from just in front of his right ear across his cheek to the corner of his mouth. Otherwise he had a face as calm and untroubled as that of a small child.

"Elliott Stark?" Dillon spoke the name bluntly.

"Ah yes, the enigmatic Mr Stark. Tell me, why the interest in him? When you called you didn't say," he spoke quietly as he continued to pack away his laptop and files.

Before Dillon could reply, the door they had entered the theatre through slammed shut with a loud bang. The three men looked round at the same time, Klein looked panicky.

"I think I should make it absolutely transparent before we go any further, Mr Klein, that what we discuss will stay confidential. Elliott Stark is of immense interest to the British government." Dillon said gravely.

Klein didn't appear perturbed in the slightest. "Okay, please continue."

"You were held in the same Beijing detention centre as Elliott Stark. I'm curious to hear on what grounds the Chinese held you and how well you got to know him?"

Brandon Klein zipped up his laptop carry bag with a slight, abstracted frown and sighed. "As a matter of fact, I don't consider that anyone ever knows Elliott Stark. He is a man who leaves you wondering. In the time we were held at that detention centre there was one thing I became sure of."

"Which was?"

"Stark is most definitely not what he promoted himself to be. Firstly, he was treated differently by the Chinese guards. I watched them when they were around him, they were frightened of him."

"But why were the guards frightened of Stark?"

"My belief is that Stark wasn't being detained. He was in the detention centre of his own volition and by the order of someone high up in the committee."

"What reason was he there?" Klasson asked.

"The word was that he was being held on drug smuggling charges."

"Have you mentioned this to anyone else?" Dillon asked.

"No one ever asked me."

Dillon nodded. "Okay, tell me whatever you can."

"Well, I entered China by invitation of the university to give a series of lectures. I was supposed to stay for five days but on the third day I was arrested by Chinese intelligence. I was taken to their headquarters and interrogated for forty-eight hours on suspicion of spying."

"What reason did they give for arresting you?"

"They didn't."

"The Chinese way of doing things." Dillon commented.

"Do you think that Stark could have been looking for someone inside the detention centre?"

"Possibly, he was allowed access to every zone of the complex, while we were confined to the one block away from other prisoners." Klein held Dillon's gaze. "Now gentlemen, if you have no further questions I have to be somewhere else." He picked up his case and left the lecture theatre.

"I think we should keep a close eye on Mr Klein. He'd been prepped by someone of our visit and I didn't believe a word he said."

* * *

Dillon drove the Porsche Panamera back across town towards Sandbanks. On the way Klasson asked. "Do you think it's possible that Stark was in the detention centre to meet someone?"

"If you've got enough money to burn, it can make everything is possible," Dillon laughed gently.

"Klein is right, there's more to Stark than meets the eye," Klasson said thoughtfully.

The high metal gates automatically opened as Dillon approached the luxury waterside house on the Sandbanks peninsular, closing silently behind them as parked on the driveway. Rumple came outside where Dillon briefed him on Klein as they walked.

"Tell London that we need two teams to cover twenty-four-hour surveillance on Klein - today."

"I'll get on it straight away," Rumple said as he walked back.

* * *

Sir Hector Blackwood listened to what Dillon had to say, a strange abstracted look on his face. "I've spoken to Interpol while you were gone."

"Renzo Montanari?"

Sir Hector nodded. "It's curiously disturbing, Dillon. There is an uncomfortable lack of information on him. Now that sets off the alarm bells for me. It's one thing knowing that a criminal mastermind or organised crime syndicate is involved but this whole state of affairs with Elliott Stark is a complete poser, too many loose ends and dead ends. How do you see it?"

Dillon stood up and paced backwards and forwards across the room. "Let's take the two most important factors. Firstly, is this Chinese man, Feng? We know that he is an enforcer for the Macau crime syndicate—the Triads are extremely dangerous killers with links to terrorist organisations in the Middle and Far East. Secondly, Elliott Stark flew to China to meet someone inside the walls of a high security detention centre. It must have been something extremely serious for him to do this because these are not places anyone goes visiting without a very good reason. That still leaves us with the most puzzling bit. Why should a wealthy businessman such as Renzo Montanari be involved with smugglers, criminals and terrorists? There's another point, this racket Stark's running with these Guernsey fishermen, so amateurish it's laughable. Montanari must have another hidden agenda for his involvement."

"Right, so you think Stark's organisation is amateurish. But I believe it's the opposite, especially with the Chinese being involved. As for Montanari, I don't know. Of course, it's always possible that the Chinese haven't realised how second-rate Stark's set-up is."

"You could be right," Dillon mused. "But the Chinese are complex, they are experts in the art of building networks of smugglers all over the world - so why is Stark involved? There must be something in his past we're not seeing. I suspect that's how they got Montanari involved, they know something of his past dealings."

Sir Hector sat there staring into space for twenty seconds and then he nodded. "Right, Dillon, it's your assignment. Find them; the three of them. Feng, Stark and Montanari, I want to know what it is they're up to but most importantly, I want them stopped."

"Stopped? Sir Hector."

"Naturally, but your methods do tend to leave a trail of

corpses behind you! The Home Secretary wants them to be taken alive. I personally can't see any point in taking half measures. It's completely up to you how you play it based on how much resistance you meet. Use the usual communication channels whenever possible to keep me informed. See Miss Young and she'll arrange your field equipment. Any questions?"

Dillon nodded. "The two officers you have watching this man Garrick at Wareham quay - pull them off the job."

"You're going there yourself?"

"I want to ask him a few questions - yes."

Sir Hector reached for his phone. "I'll see to it right away. Good luck."

Phoebe Young glanced through from the spacious open-plan living room as Dillon emerged from the study and joined her.

"So, tell. How much did Sir Hector concede?"

"You know I can't share classified information of an on-going investigation to anyone without the necessary clearance level." Dillon winked and smiled warmly at her as he walked across the highly polished Travertine floor to the wall of glass bi-folding doors. He opened one and stepped out into the south facing garden that went to the water's edge. Once outside, he lit a cigarette, went to end of the garden and gazed over the world's largest natural harbour. He stood thinking of his next move, occasionally smoking the cigarette, his eyes as dark as the devil's.

Phoebe Young came and stood beside him.

"What is it, Jake?"

"I'm not sure," he said. "I'm more personally involved with this assignment than any other I've worked on in a long time. I'm trying to work out why the old man Chen Chi-li, or Chang the name he was travelling under, was left to drown. I tried to save him but the current was too fierce that morning and it took him. We had to leave him on the beach. It doesn't matter that he was the head of the Macau crime syndicate, in the end he only wanted to see his only son."

He sighed heavily and stubbed out his cigarette. "For the first time in my career I am taking it personally that someone has tried to have me killed on two separate occasions. So much so that I intend to take care of that someone permanently for purely selfish reasons. It's part of the job, of course. But what worries me is that I am looking forward to it."

* * *

He had said goodbye to Erik Klasson with regret, for he had come to admire the brilliant, sardonic Scandinavian - and not only because of what they had been through together. He was being ordered back to Sweden to start another investigation. Klasson was in Dillon's study, he was wearing a pair of Dillon's trousers, a role-neck sweater and a Barbour jacket.

Dillon zipped up the lightweight Kevlar bullet proof vest and then put on a black military style field jacket over it. "I don't suppose I'll be seeing you again. By this evening you'll be back in Sweden."

"Good luck. When you next see Stark, please give him everything he deserves." Erik Klasson grinned and held out his hand. "Good luck Jake Dillon."

Dillon had the door half-open when Klasson spoke again. "Just one thing that's been nagging at me. Why do you think they killed Bergfalk in that way?"

"I can only guess. The Tide Runner was being shadowed by the UK coastguard and in danger of being boarded. Stark couldn't risk Bergfalk being found on-board, he panicked and decided to get rid of the evidence."

Erik Klasson laughed. "You know something, Alek Bergfalk was a very dangerous man—ironic isn't it, that Elliott Stark killed him with a garrotte? It was the way that Bergfalk liked to kill his victims."

He laughed again but this time there was no humour. "Look after yourself."

Dillon closed the door gently and stood thinking of Elliott Stark.

Chapter 11

Wareham Quay
Dorset
UK

The Porsche Panamera entered the historic market town of Wareham with Dillon behind the wheel.

He drove to the far end of the high street. Just before the bridge running over the River Frome, he turned into a narrow side street finding somewhere to park at the side of the road. Then walked to the quay and scanned the vicinity to get his bearings.

People milled around the lively riverside quay with its local pubs and restaurants. But he wasn't there to wine and dine; he was there to find Garrick and after forty-five minutes of waiting his patience had worn thin. He stood up and walked into the Quay Inn. At the bar he ordered a coffee, chatting to the friendly barmaid.

"I'm looking for a friend of mine. His name is Garrick."

"Oh, you know Garrick do you? Well, you won't find that rogue here today or any other day."

"This is his local though?"

"Yeah, until the immature bugger got himself barred by the landlord."

"Why?"

"Because of something he said to Garrick who took offence and broke the landlord's nose which I found as funny as hell." She laughed.

"Do you know where I can find him?" Dillon sipped his coffee.

"He lives Swanage way. You might find him in the bar of The Black Swan Inn on the High Street."

"Thanks, you've been very helpful."

"I'm Nici. If I can be of further help, you know where I am," she said with a smile and a crafty wink.

Dillon smiled and left the bar.

* * *

Dillon approached the coastal town from Langton Matravers on the A351, following the road into the centre of Swanage.

The high street seemed quiet with few people around. They hurried for cover as a frigid, blustery wind whipped against everything solid, houses, cars and trees. Overhead the sky had turned tar black and large clouds moved inland fast, then came the rain, hard pelting, lashing against the ground. Dillon parked the Porsche, sitting in the dry warm interior while he waited for the torrential downpour to subside.

The storm passed over the town leaving the smell of dampness hanging in the air. Dillon walked up the high street to the pub the barmaid had said Garrick frequented when he was around Swanage. He moved inside, reappearing a moment later with Garrick's whereabouts during the day.

* * *

The boatyard wasn't hard to find a mile west of Swanage Bay and a ghost of a place. A graveyard of optimism and water going craft that had lost their battle with age and the elements. The office of sorts stood in front of a decaying timber-built bungalow. There didn't appear to be anyone around so he moved towards the jetty.

Tied up alongside the rickety timber jetty was a sea-going inflatable rib with a fibreglass hull. The six Yamaha 2-stroke V6 outboard motors at the stern giving combined power of two thousand horsepower.

There was an enclosed wheelhouse and enough capacity for twenty people on deck. An interesting craft, Dillon thought. Rigged out for sea fishing with two swivel chairs bolted to the stern deck along with an electric steel wired hoist, even more interesting.

This looked expensive; there was no doubt of that. He

stood for a while staring at the six outboard motors strapped to the stern, then turned away.

A man stood a short distance away observing him from the shadow of an old barge. He was six feet three inches tall and of slender build, dressed in an army surplus full-length trench coat, black beanie hat, jeans and a heavy knit jumper. At first glance he had a face you'd forget even while you're looking at it. But as he got closer Dillon could make out the grey under the edge of the hat, grey lips and grey eyes. His face expressionless, the eyes behind the round gunmetal spectacles, empty.

"Admiring the boat, are you?" His voice did not fit with what he was wearing and as he approached, Dillon at once noticed the clean manicured hands and nails, again contradicting the clothing he was wearing.

"Yeah, she looks a fast one all right. What's it got, thousand horses?"

"Double that and a tad more when the nitrous flows," he boasted. "Now what are you doing here?" Public school qualities rolled off his tongue as he spoke.

Dillon ignored the question. "She's quick then and by the looks of it better equipped than those luxury boats in Poole Harbour. I mean, look at that multi-screen head unit on the console and that's the latest GPS Sat-Nav there. There's sonar and radar, it's very impressive." Dillon said, adding. "I'm looking for a man named Garrick."

"You know boats then?"

"A little, are you Garrick?"

"That's right. What can I do for you?"

"I'd need to take a trip - if your boat is for hire that is?"

"You want to go fishing?" Garrick shook his head. "It's too late in the day now."

"I'm thinking of more than that," Dillon said. "The fact is, I need to get across the Channel in a hurry. A friend of mine told me you might oblige at a price."

Garrick looked towards the water. "Who is this friend?" he asked, after a short pause.

Dillon looked embarrassed. "He wasn't a friend. Just a bloke I met in a bar in Covent Garden. He said any time I wanted to get out of the country in a hurry, you were the man to see."

Garrick spun and spoke over his shoulder as he walked

away. "Come up to the office. It'll be raining soon."

Dillon followed him and mounted the wobbly wooden steps to the office. At the top, he paused and turned his head, aware of movement by the derelict boats. Was he imagining it or was it a dog? But whatever it might have been, it left him with a vague unease as he walked inside the office.

The place was a bombsite, filthy dirty with files and payment demands scattered around on every surface and on the floor. Garrick used his arm to sweep off the clutter from his desk and produced a bottle of Vodka and two shot glasses.

"So, you want to get across the water as fast as possible, do you?" he said.

Dillon placed his holdall on the desk and unzipped it. He retrieved a transparent plastic wallet containing five thousand pounds sterling. Garrick's eyes fixed on the bundle.

Dillon pushed the wallet towards Garrick. "There's five thousand sterling there. You'll get another five when we get across the water. Do we have an agreement, Garrick?"

Garrick's smile exposed gleaming white teeth, another contradiction in terms of his general look, Dillon thought. Garrick scooped up the wallet and pushed it into his overcoat pocket. "When do you want to leave?"

"The sooner the better."

Garrick smiled a wicked smile. "Then why are we waiting? The tide is perfect, and the weather settled." He got up and going outside led the way.

* * *

The boat was every bit as good as she looked. Dillon stood at the rail as they moved through the Channel from the boatyard towards the open sea breathing in the salt air. It felt good being on the water again, even towards the uncertainty of what was ahead. But that's the job, not knowing what's around the corner or if you'd still be alive the next day.

Waves slapped against the rigid hull making the whole boat shudder. As they left the shelter of the natural harbour Garrick increased the power, lifting the bow as they raced towards open sea.

Garrick increased their speed up to forty-five knots and Dillon moved to the wheelhouse and entered its shelter. He closed the door behind him and with it the wind and noise coming from the six V6 Yamaha outboard motors.

"You weren't kidding when you said it was a fast boat, so how long until we reach the French coast?"

"If we keep this pace and get a tad more out of her, we should pass the Channel Islands in two hours. The French coast half an hour later."

"Where were you thinking of putting me ashore?"

"Anywhere you say," Garrick said. "You're the boss."

"I want to stay away from ports and tourist centres, so head for the Bay of Lannion on the Brittany coast."

"Suits me, if the tide is right I can get you up the creek and drop you there."

Garrick altered course by two degrees and Dillon said, "I'll sit by the bulkhead and keep out of your way. Let me know when we're passing the Channel Islands."

"Best if you sleep now. Could get rough in mid-Channel, if you want coffee there's a thermos flask in that bag." Garrick pointed to a rucksack in the corner.

Dillon felt tired, which was not surprising. He poured himself a coffee and sitting, leaned back against the bulkhead and drank the hot black liquid, going over the assignment point by point. Garrick was spoiling for a fight but not just yet; that could wait until later.

Dillon shook his head, hadn't realised how tired he was, trying his best to stay awake. And then his brain was ceasing to function. God, he felt exhausted. He stretched out on the wheelhouse floor using his holdall as a pillow and stared up at the roof. His eyes were so heavy now, he felt hot and his throat and mouth had become dry. It was only in the final moment of his plunge headfirst into the darkness he realised that Garrick had drugged the coffee.

* * *

Surfacing from the effect of the sleeping pills, head pounding, as if he'd been drinking cheap whisky on a weekend bender, he only felt his basic life support functions, heart beating and the ability to breathe unaided. Trying to get up, he felt the cable ties bite into his wrists.

The rib was still moving at speed, the outboard motors

sending vibrations through the fibreglass hull. Dillon lay on the floor of the wheelhouse, Garrick sitting at the wheel. Dillon rolled over, the restraints around his wrists making it difficult to stand up.

Garrick glanced at Dillon and reduced the power to idle. The nose of the craft dipped, he squatted so close that Dillon became at once aware of the rancid smell of sour breath and sweat from his unwashed body.

"How's your head, then?" Garrick patted his cheek.

"What's this, Garrick?" Dillon demanded, staying with his role for the time being. "I thought we'd agreed."

Garrick got up and opened Dillon's holdall, which was now on a shelf on the starboard side of the wheelhouse. He took out a sealed packet of bank notes. "This is the game mate, hard currency. I've always craved for the stuff; it makes me tingle. What you've got in here will keep me going for months and I've grown attached to it."

"Okay," Dillon said. "I won't give you any trouble. Just drop me off on the French coast as agreed and we'll call it quits."

Garrick's laugh was derisory as he cut the restraining ropes around his ankles, hauled him to his feet and pushed him through the door. "I'll drop you off. In fact, this is a good time for you to go for a swim."

It was freezing outside on the deck, rain drifting through the failing light. Dillon turned to face him. Garrick now had a baseball bat in his right hand, swinging it by his leg. Dillon said, "Who taught you this little trick, Elliott Stark?"

It stopped Garrick in his tracks. He attempted to compose himself but was unnerved by the mention of Stark's name. His eyes had narrowed and when he spoke his voice was the merest whisper.

"Who are you? What is this?"

"It's no good, Garrick," Dillon told him point-blank. "When I don't turn up in France, someone will give you a visit."

"I'm supposed to quake in my boots, am I?"

"Oh, there won't be any time for that, Garrick. The person they send looking for me will have one reason for being there. To kill you."

Garrick's next reaction was erratic. He raised the baseball bat and swung it around as intimidation until he drew his arm back to strike but the bat never came forward. A hand emerged from behind and wrenched the bat from his grasp. Garrick spun round and Erik Klasson stepped forward and struck him with enough force to put him on the deck.

Garrick didn't hesitate. His hand disappeared under his jacket and reappeared grasping the butt of a snub-nosed Smith & Wesson revolver but he made the mistake of pulling the trigger instead of squeezing it. The bullet ploughed into the wheelhouse and Erik Klasson dropped to the deck and had slithered to the other side for cover. There was a long-handled gaff used for pulling in large game fish, secured by spring clips on the side of the wheelhouse. As he pulled it free, one clip twanged and Garrick turned. Klasson had the gaff in his hands.

This time he was on his feet and more composed. His arm swung up in a straight line as he sighted the barrel. Dillon lowered his frame, rugby style, sending him staggering to the rail. The Smith & Wesson went off and Garrick straightened, aiming at Dillon's chest.

Klasson came out of the darkness, lunging at Garrick with the gaff, the point catching him between the ribs on his right side. He flipped over the side backwards. By the time Dillon got there, the black water had consumed him.

"Hold out your hands," Klasson ordered and sliced through Dillon's bonds with the edge of the razor-sharp gaff.

Dillon turned, massaging his wrists to restore circulation. "I've never been so glad to see anyone as I am to see you. Where the hell were you hiding?"

"I'm glad you're glad, Dillon." Klasson said. "After you'd left, I thought things through for five minutes then got Mr Rumple to track your implanted chip. He drove me in one of your cars to that shabby little boatyard. We arrived minutes after you."

"What happened next?"

"Oh, I hid amongst those old wrecks just below the boatyard office."

"It was you I spotted." Dillon said.

"Yeah, I thought Garrick had spotted me but you thought it was a cat you'd seen and Garrick ignored you - lucky for me. I heard most of your conversation with him, waited till you'd gone into the office, then got on board and hid under a tarpaulin."

"Well, you certainly cut your entrance fine, or possibly that was your Swedish sense of the dramatic?"

"As a matter of fact, I fell asleep and didn't wake up till I heard Garrick making that noise."

Dillon eyed the Swede suspiciously. "Okay, but what are you doing here. You're supposed to be in Stockholm?"

"It's simple. I called my department controller, told him I was taking a week's leave while I was in the UK. I want to see Stark's face when he finds out we're still on his case," Klasson laughed.

"I'm cool with that," Dillon said, as they went back inside the wheelhouse. "Let's get moving again and get to the French coast." Dillon added.

Erik Klasson nodded and perched himself on the bulkhead. The outboard motors burst into life and the rib lurched forward as Dillon pushed up the throttle and with a burst of power they headed towards the French coast.

Chapter 12

**Brittany Coast
Northern France**

They passed the Channel Island of Jersey doing fifty knots; the rib cutting through the calm water towards the Brittany coast fifty miles away. Dillon kept a watchful eye on the depth sounder as he altered course to avoid the danger lurking just below the surface. The rib leaned over as he threw the craft around jutting rocks that could rip the fiberglass hull wide open.

They made the French coast by nine-thirty that evening and the stretch of coast with Stark's hotel. Dillon checked the charts and spotted a small bay with an inlet leading to what could be a canal or river a quarter of a mile to the east. Dillon gave it a go.

He couldn't have made a better choice. The bay was a perfect circle, only two hundred yards in diameter and guarded by high cliffs which gave excellent cover from the sea. He reduced their speed to a mere crawl as they entered the mouth of the inlet, using only two out of the six Yamaha outboard motors.

The channel narrowed to nothing more than a stream after a hundred yards with thick vegetation to one side and open fields on the other. Dillon came alongside what was once a wooden jetty, now only odd timbers poking out of the water similar to rotten teeth. Klasson tied the stern line to one timber while Dillon dropped the anchor.

Dillon grabbed his holdall from inside the wheelhouse. Out came the false bottom showing a secret compartment that held three weapons. A Glock 20 along with a Magpul FMG-9 submachine gun and Dillon's new weapon, the Armatix Ip1 pistol with a fingerprint recognition trigger.

Klasson looked on as Dillon took the weapons from their hiding place and ensured each had a round in the chamber and full magazine clip.

"What is this?" Klasson asked in amazement.

"It's called being prepared, Erik," Dillon said handing him the Glock and four extra clips. He dropped the 9mm handgun into one of his jacket pockets and the other clips into another.

Dillon removed a shoulder holster from the holdall, put it on under his jacket, then placed the Armatix into it. The Magpul machine pistol slipped inside the lining of the tailored jacket to conceal the weapon and enable quick access to it. He deposited four stun grenades, one in each of his outer pockets. He replaced the false bottom into the holdall and stowed it back inside the bulkhead of the wheelhouse.

They both stepped up onto land. "Now for the most interesting part of this evening," Dillon said.

They moved off at a jog back towards the bay and ascended the narrow path leading to the top of the cliffs. The sky ranged from perfect blue-black to millions of sparkling diamonds. There was no moonlight yet a strange luminosity hung over everything, giving them a range of vision under the circumstances much greater than expected. They made fast progress through scattered pines and soon came to a point from which they could see Stark's hotel.

There were lights on in several windows of the hotel.

"So, Dillon, what's your plan?" Klasson whispered.

"What plan? I don't have a plan, we play this one by ear," Dillon told him. "Let's see how many guests are at the party first."

They moved from the hill and the clifftop at a steady pace, using the cover of the pine forest, following a narrow track cut between the trees. The road ran parallel to the forest and right past the rear of the hotel. They were a hundred yards away from their target. Moving fast along the quiet unlit road and as they approached the hotel, Klasson held Dillon's sleeve. "Stark may have placed lookouts or electronic sensors around the place, or had you thought of that?"

Dillon looked at the Swedish intelligence officer. "We'd better be careful then."

They covered the ground in a flash, staying tight to the verge until they reached a low stone wall. They had a perfect view into the rear windows of the hotel at the far end of the vegetable garden.

"Come on, let's get closer." Dillon rolled over the wall landing in soft earth, Klasson followed him.

They crept around the edge of the garden, keeping low to the wall until they reached the other end, crouching below the first window. Light reached out with golden fingers into the darkness, Dillon could hear the persistent drip-drip-drip of a leaking tap coming from the cracked open kitchen window.

Dillon peered through a gap in the half raised blind, saw Dan Lacroix, Finnegan's first mate from the Tide Runner, sitting at the kitchen table. He had his head bowed, a bottle of Vodka and a shot glass in front of him.

"He doesn't seem to be too happy," Klasson breathed.

Dillon nodded. "He doesn't but then he has things on his mind. A daughter who needs expensive lifesaving treatment in Switzerland or she won't see her eighth birthday."

"How sad, so young."

"That's why he's working for Stark and Finnegan, to raise the two hundred thousand Euros required for the procedure."

"So, what's our next move?" Klasson asked.

"You stay out of sight and watch my back. I'll handle Lacroix."

Dillon knocked on the door of the kitchen. Lacroix was slow in responding and his footsteps dragged across the flagstone floor. He opened the door and peered out, took a step forward, an anxious, hopeful expression on his face. Dillon touched the barrel of the Armatix pistol to his temple.

"You make a noise and you're a dead man, Mr Lacroix. Now get back," Dillon prodded him in the stomach.

Lacroix moved backwards and Dillon went after him, Klasson followed close. He closed the door and Lacroix looked from one to the other than laughed.

"This'll be a surprise for Finnegan and Stark. They told me you were both dead."

"Where are they?" Dillon asked demanded.

"They're at a bar up the coast entertaining those two Chinese, Feng and Mingyu, along with the lady."

"Where is Dubois and his wife?" Dillon asked.

"They're asleep in their quarters on the other side of the hotel."

"Which bar?" Klasson asked.

Lacroix shrugged. "They came back here this morning in the Englishman's boat and left with the tide two hours later. There is one thing though; the Chinese man had bandages across the face."

Dillon thought for a moment and decided not to question the comment.

"Why aren't you with them?" Dillon asked suspiciously.

"I'm waiting for someone to arrive."

"Who is this someone?" Dillon demanded.

"I don't know. I'm not told names, just to look after these people when they arrive and to make sure they're comfortable until Stark returns to take them across the Channel."

"Do you know when this someone is arriving?" Klasson asked.

"I do not understand." Lacroix rubbed his eyes with the back of his hand.

"How was the lady?" Dillon enquired.

"How do you expect? She had turned out as immaculate as ever and looking stunning."

"I don't mean that. Did she appear afraid, afraid of Stark?"

Lacroix shook his head. "She looked at him as if he were..."

He appeared to have trouble finding the right word. "As if he were..."

"What?" Klasson said.

"A God - that's what." Lacroix blurted.

His composed demeanour and unafraid attitude was a challenge but the answers came in the end. Dillon let it go for the moment. "Where did they go?"

"I haven't got the slight idea."

Dillon lifted the barrel of the Armatix pistol he was still holding. "You need to consider your answer, Lacroix. Try Hades Keep for a start and Montanari, don't tell me you've never heard of them?"

"I've heard of those two names, snatches of conversations between Finnegan and Stark but nothing else. They are names and nothing more."

He was speaking the truth; Dillon knew, which didn't appear to make any sense.

"What's happened Lacroix?" he whispered. "You're a different man."

Lacroix looked up from the table. "I am a different man. My daughter died last week." The words came with tears rolling over his cheeks.

"I'm sorry for your loss Lacroix." Dillon said with genuine sadness in his voice.

Lacroix looked at Dillon. "Not a day without pain for two of her seven years and yet she never once complained. She was a baby and yet she knew there could be only one end. I tried everything. Expensive doctors from Paris and the latest drugs from America, for nothing."

"That must have cost a serious sum of money?"

Lacroix nodded. "How else do you think I came to be working for that animal Finnegan? It was for my Angelique - only Angelique. It was for her I have endured so much horror. For her and her alone that I kept my mouth shut."

"You're saying you joined them out of fear of your own life?" Klasson asked.

Lacroix shook his head, "No, fear for my daughter's life; of what that devil Stark might do to her."

"He made threats? Klasson asked.

"Yes, to keep me quiet. He had to, after a trip a few weeks ago when I sailed on the Tide Runner as a deckhand."

"What happened then?" Dillon said.

Lacroix hesitated and Dillon pressed, "Let me tell you what happened after we left here yesterday. They scuttled the Tide Runner and she sunk three miles off the Dorset coast, did Finnegan tell you that?"

"He said there had been an accident. That the engine had exploded and that the rest of you were dead."

"Well, Finnegan and Stark left us to drown, locked below deck," Klasson said. "The woman and the two Chinese went with them and the old man died trying to get ashore."

Lacroix looked shocked. "My God, they are animals, not men. Why, only the other week on the occasion I was speaking of earlier, we were just off the English coast on a border patrol boat. We had only one passenger on-board, a special trip they told me." He turned to Klasson. "He was a Scandinavian man, who had travelled overland Africa."

Klasson's face had tightened, nothing noticeable but Dillon spotted it and at once asked Lacroix.

"What happened?"

"Stark said we'd get at least seven years if caught with him on board. So, he got him up on deck…" he paused. "And then he cut his throat with that wire he pulls out of his watch when he's thinking of something. Then he put him over the side. We were in a thick fog, so the body disappeared at once. Sometimes I can still see the terror in his eyes when Stark was cutting open his throat with that wire."

Dillon nodded. "And he told you he'd kill your daughter the same way if you didn't keep quiet."

"That's right."

Klasson turned and left. Lacroix looked bewildered and Dillon whispered, "He knew the dead man well Lacroix. We're here to settle the account. Will you help us?"

Lacroix took a waterproof jacket from behind the door. "I'm in, whatever it takes."

"Good. In that case wait here until Stark and the others return. Have you seen the skipper of the Sea Dragon today?"

"He was here yesterday."

"Where is he now?" Dillon asked.

"He sailed back to Guernsey, I believe."

"That's good. It means he's out of the way, so we can use that to our gain." Dillon said. "Now, when Stark and the others return, I want you to tell him that the Sea Dragon is returning here, and the skipper needs to talk to him. Make sure the others overhear you tell him this."

"What happens after this?"

"You text the skipper and instruct him to return to Brittany at once as Stark wants to go over something straightaway. You might add that Stark's phone has no signal here, and that's why you're contacting him, understand?"

"Yes."

"Do you have a boat here?"

Lacroix nodded. "There is a dinghy with an outboard motor in the harbour. I can use that."

"Good, when we leave you will go back up the hill and over to the Bay of Lannion. You know it?"

"I know every inch of this coast."

"We'll wait for you there," Dillon said, adding, "and don't worry; we will fix him and the bully Finnegan, eh, Lacroix?"

Lacroix's eyes glowed with fire, the hatred boiling over as they walked outside together.

* * *

Lacroix left to check that the Duboises had gone to bed in their private quarters. Then positioned himself at a window in the bar that gave him a view of the small harbour and beach.

He didn't have to wait too long before he spotted Stark's power cruiser coming alongside the jetty. The low throb from the inboard diesel engine was audible as Stark manoeuvred the thirty-eight-foot boat into position. Finnegan was on the jetty tying off the forward and stern lines. *I will make sure you get what's due to you!* Lacroix thought. He smiled not a nice smile but one filled with pure hatred.

Stark entered the bar with Camille De Rosa and Mingyu on his arm either side of him, followed by Finnegan and Feng. Stark was holding court with the women, laughing with them but Dan Lacroix knew better than being conned by his act.

"Ah, Lacroix - good to see you're still awake. Pour us a drink," Finnegan ordered.

Lacroix poured the finest French Cognac from a cut crystal decanter into five brandy snifter glasses while Feng looked on, tension on his face.

It was Finnegan who stood up and proposed a toast. "To wealth and freedom, may there both be plenty."

They looked at him and then Stark looked around the room at each of them before laughing. Lacroix remained behind the bar looking bewildered but he would deliver the message Dillon had instructed him to give Stark and Finnegan.

"First thing tomorrow I will be away with the tide and you'll never see me again." Finnegan's speech gave every sign of him being drunk. Lacroix had never seen him drunk in the three years he'd known him.

"Before I forget Mr Stark, the Sea Dragon is returning here as the skipper needs to talk to you straightaway."

"Why didn't he call me?" Stark demanded.

"No service on his mobile, he phoned me before he left Guernsey."

Stark had his smartphone in his hand speed dialling the skipper's number. Lacroix sighed relief as the No Service message came over the loud speaker.

"What does the skipper want I wonder?" Finnegan asked in his Irish brogue.

"He should arrive soon." Lacroix said.

"Did he say what he wanted? Is it trouble, maybe it's a problem with the boat?"

Lacroix shrugged. "Captain Finnegan, he told me nothing."

Finnegan glared at him in surprise, aware of a new belligerence in his tone but there was no time to question him now.

"I'll be leaving you now, Mr Stark, I'll sleep on your boat tonight and make sure everything is checked and ready for the morning," Lacroix said and started for the door.

"You're going to the boat now?" Finnegan asked.

"That's right."

"I'll come with you to talk things through with you now. I'm leaving."

Lacroix nodded, "If you must."

Lacroix faded out of the bar and into the night and was glad to be away from Stark at last. He distrusted Finnegan, there wasn't a hint of drunkenness in his manner. Lacroix felt uneasy for the first time in his miserable life, for he looked even more dangerous than usual. Leaving through the courtyard they took the steps to the jetty.

Finnegan at once spotted the Sea Dragon moored alongside the jetty behind Stark's power cruiser. Its engines whispering but the boat looked deserted. Finnegan pushed Lacroix out of the way as he lumbered forward and up the ladder to the deck, pausing uneasily. There was movement below deck and he descended the companionway towards the sound.

"You there skipper, it's Finnegan?" he demanded.

As he reached the door, his heart felt as if had stopped beating. A face stared at him from the darkness. Disembodied by the single flame from a match igniting a cigarette, was one face he had never expected to see again in this life.

Dillon smiled smoothly. "Come in, Finnegan."

Finnegan stepped back and the muzzle of a Glock touched him in the nape of his neck. He turned his head as the lights were switched on and looked straight at Erik Klasson.

Sweat sprang to his forehead, and he felt a shiver run up and down his spine, as if death had walked through him. What he was seeing could not be possible. He sagged against the bulkhead with a groan.

The Sea Dragon left the jetty and moved out to sea.

* * *

By the time Dillon had travelled up the coast, sailed around in circles for a while and then returned to Lannion Bay where the Sea Dragon dropped anchor Finnegan no longer believed in ghosts. His earlier surprise had been traded for anger and now he awaited his chance to strike.

It came when Lacroix arrived and tied up alongside in the dinghy. Klasson caught the line he threw, leaving Dillon at the wheel concentrating on keeping the Sea Dragon from smashing the small dinghy on the large swell. Finnegan seized his opportunity by lurching forward towards Dillon who had expected such a move. He spun round on the seat and with little effort side stepped a wild punch before grasping the Irishman's throat.

"So big man, you thought you had a chance!" Dillon chided and tightened his grip so that Finnegan nearly passed out.

Dillon released his grip on the Irishman and slammed him into the bulkhead with a hefty punch to his oversized gut. The blow would have doubled up any other man, sending him to his knees for several minutes. Finnegan rolled one shoulder, came to his feet and lunged for Dillon in a pure rage. Klasson had re-entered the wheelhouse and got a foot under him in time. Finnegan fell sprawling on to the deck.

When he got to his feet, he found Dillon smiling sneeringly and Klasson taking off his jacket. "Come on then bully-boy, let's see how tough you really are Finnegan," he said.

"I'll rip off your fucking head."

Finnegan came in, a charging rhinoceros. Arms outstretched, fisted hands held in boxing posture advancing fast. Only to get the beating of his life as Klasson demolished him with blow after blow, the exactitude of skill was awe-inspiring in its economy. The Swede in action was something to see and his calm collected state of mind gave him the edge.

Every punch Finnegan threw only touched air. In return, he exposed himself to a barrage of blows that were devastating in their effect. Sending the big Irishman to his knees again and again until a final back hand punch put him on his back.

He lay there gasping for breath and Klasson dropped to one knee beside him. "And now, Finnegan you will answer my questions without pissing me off."

Finnegan spat in his face and Dillon put a bullet in his leg. He screamed as the bullet smashed bone and ripped tissue apart as it made a messy and gory exit just behind the knee.

"You fucking bastards, who are you, what do you want?"

Dillon pulled up Klasson. "Take a breath of fresh air out on deck. Let me try." He lit a cigarette. "We hate you, Finnegan - the Swede because you messed up his investigation when you killed Bergfalk, Lacroix because you dragged him into the filth with you. And me, because you smell and have no manners. You are something from under a stone and I'd no more hesitate to kill you than step on a cockroach. Now you know where you are in the chain, we'll try again. Who does Stark answer too?"

Finnegan's reply was what Dillon was expecting. "Fuck you."

Dillon stood up, grabbed hold of the Irishman's coat collar and dragged him outside screaming with the searing pain in his leg. Lacroix booted Finnegan hard in the ribs "You heard the man."

Finnegan groaned and rolled over on his back, his eyes full of venom.

Dillon tossed Klasson a coil of nylon rope. "Tie his wrists."

Finnegan didn't bother to struggle. "You can do whatever, you won't make me talk. I'll see you in hell first."

He ranted on for a time but Dillon ignored him and walked to the stern where he studied the rail.

"Let's have him here."

Klasson dragged Finnegan to the stern where Dillon hauled him up onto his feet. With no preamble Dillon tied off the free end of the rope to the rear rail and was feeding it overboard. Klasson and Lacroix grabbed the Irishman and one fluid action sent him over the side and into the water head first.

Finnegan surfaced, cursing Dillon while trying to keep his head above the surface.

"Are you ready to talk, Finnegan?"

"I'll see you in hell first."

Dillon nodded; Klasson entered the wheelhouse and a moment later the inboard diesel engine started. The forward anchor was winched in, and the cruiser powered out of the bay.

Watching from the stern rail, Dillon waited for the rope tied to the Irishman's wrists to catch and then Finnegan disappeared beneath the surface, hauled behind the boat at speed. Dillon gave him a full minute, checking his Omega watch before he gave Klasson the signal to stop. Lacroix helped Dillon pull the rope back in with Finnegan coughing and spluttering, his chest heaving as he sobbed for breath. He coughed and then vomited. Dillon gave him a moment to recover.

"Hades Keep, Montanari, I want you to tell what and who they are?"

Finnegan remained unhelpful. Dillon rounded and signalled to go again, his face unemotional, the rope uncoiled again.

This time he made it one minute and a half and when Finnegan appeared there was scarcely any movement. Dillon pulled the rope back on board. Klasson came to the stern and helped Lacroix haul the Irishman back on board. Dillon knelt beside him and after a while the great head lifted and the eyes opened.

'Hades Keep,' he croaked. "It's a house in the Briere National Park near a village called Saint Joachim, Montanari owns it."

"And that's where Stark and the others are going?" Finnegan nodded. "And Montanari is he there now?"

"Don't know I never met him and only know what Stark has told me."

"Why were you not going with the others?"

"Stark wanted me to take care of Lacroix, he knows too much and he wanted him shut up for good. When I'd done the job, I was to leave for Ireland at once."

"So, you were to kill Lacroix? Well, you've failed captain. Haven't you?" Dillon said.

Finnegan coughed, then gave a strange choking cry. His body heaved as if he was in pain and Klasson and Lacroix knelt beside him untying his hands. Lacroix lowered his head and put his ear against Finnegan's chest. When he looked up, his face was grave.

"He's dead. It looks as if his heart has given out."

"Let's hope he told the truth then," Dillon said coolly. "Get him into a cabin."

He turned and Klasson grabbed him by the arm. "Is that the only thing you can say? We've just killed a man."

Dillon lowered his gaze to Klasson's hand, looked back up at the Swedish investigator fleetingly before saying. "One way or another he was due for it," Dillon said. "So, keep your sentimentality to yourself, I haven't got the time or the conscience for that crap."

He pulled free going into the wheelhouse. He was examining the chart on the screen when they joined him. "We need a nice deep channel," he said to Lacroix. "Deep enough for this cruiser to sink into without a trace."

Lacroix sighed. "A pity, it's such a stunning boat."

"She's got to go, Stark has to believe Finnegan has gone out to sea to kill you," Dillon said. "Where do you suggest?"

Lacroix studied the chart on the screen for a moment or two, then jabbed a finger at a group of rocks three miles out.

"These rocks have taken many ships in their time. They stick up above the surface at low tide but are unseen at high tide. The water's deep and no matter what goes there stays there, believe me."

Dillon nodded. "Lacroix, take the dinghy back up the creek. You'll see where we moored the rib and then return here in it. Klasson you go with him. When you return I'll follow?"

"I'll stay here with you." Klasson said in an unfriendly voice.

Dillon shook his head. "No point man, it's a one-man job."

"I said I'd stay." Klasson's voice was bleak. "What I say I mean."

He moved out on deck and stood with his hands in his pockets, collar turned up and shoulders hunched.

"I think he's pissed at something," Lacroix commented.

"Don't know why he should be. That bastard Irishman had it coming."

"It's what occurred before his death that's bothering him," Dillon said. "He's got a moral conscience, Lacroix. Now let's get moving. It'll take you only five minutes to get to the rib and return. We need to hurry as we have got little time."

* *   *

Dillon sighted the patches of white water in the distance. As the boats approached, the turbulence increased and Dillon knew of huge plumes of spray that became effervescent in the night.

Only just visible from the surface, jagged rocks infested the water lurking just under the surface, others stood twenty feet above the wave, lingering in wait for their next victim. When Lacroix whistled and waved, the agreed signal, Dillon cut the power and called to Klasson, who had been waiting. Now he opened the hatch to the engine compartment and returned up on deck. Dillon came out of the wheelhouse as Lacroix came alongside the cruiser in the rib which looked tiny up against the sleek power craft.

Dillon made sure Klasson was on-board the rib, before going to the top of the companionway. Retrieving a grenade from his jacket pocket he pulled the pin and dropped it into the engine compartment. As he flipped over the rail, the grenade detonated, the boat rocked intensely as its hull broke apart. Dillon landed roughly onto the deck of other boat. Lacroix powered up the six Yamaha outboard motors, the rib's nose lifted as they surged forward through the foaming spume. He took the rib round in a wide circle. Dillon and Klasson looked back as the cruiser lifted through ninety degrees and went nose first to the bottom of the deep channel. Loose debris floated on the surface of the water.

"Lost at sea," Lacroix said. "Sunk and nobody will ever see Liam Finnegan again," he said with a wide grin on his face.

"What if Finnegan's body is discovered?" Klasson asked.

Dillon shrugged. "Believe it or not, but most people who get blind drunk fall into the Channel don't turn up again. Even if he pops up and someone finds what's left of him after a few weeks it'll fit with the story."

"You have a tidy mind," Klasson said.

"As with any professional, the trick is to keep it simple."

"So, what's the plan now?" Erik Klasson demanded, as he turned in his seat, shoulders hunched against the spray.

"Now, I send Mr Rumple a message so he can arrange transport to get us to Saint Joachim." Dillon said. "I'm assuming it's still us working this assignment?"

Klasson nodded. "I'm still on holiday leave, it's too late to step back from this. You needn't worry - I'll be watching your back along the way."

"Fair enough," Dillon turned to Lacroix. "Take us along the coast and drop us near to St Malo."

"Okay, we're fifteen minutes from St Malo."

Dillon lit a cigarette and passed it to Lacroix. "Finnegan, Lacroix, there could be questions."

"Maybe, but I doubt it. He would leave in the morning. Most people will think he left early. He was observed going out to Stark's boat and where is Stark's boat now? Maybe in a few days something will be hauled into a net by a fishing boat or wreckage drift ashore somewhere. The fact is that Liam Finnegan never existed."

"And you? What will you do?"

"I will go home and bury my daughter," Lacroix said.

Chapter 13

It was just before midnight when they reached St Malo. Dillon had received a message from Rumple giving him a report of where he could find the small Citroen van that would get them to Saint Joachim.

They walked for twenty minutes from the point where Lacroix had put them ashore, to where the Citroen was. Dillon punched in the security code, the metal roller door lifted and they walked down the ramp into the private underground garage. The lights popped on as they walked past the sensors into otherwise darkness.

Dillon moved straight to the van, reaching under the wheel arch where he found the key placed on top of the front driver side wheel. Dillon threw his holdall into the back of the Citroen and wasting no time he drove up to the top of the ramp. He looked along the street either way; he was looking for anyone who might watch them come out of the garage. The street was empty.

Dillon kept within the speed limit, not wishing to bring any unwanted attention to them as they motored towards Saint Joachim. The Swedish intelligence officer sitting next to him was still brooding and had little to say for himself. Dillon had had enough and pulled over to the side of the road.

"It won't work, Klasson," he said. "Either we get things straight now or you drop out now and I'll go on alone."

"You need me for this gig," Klasson said. "Any issue I have with you, Dillon - is my problem. All you need to remember is that I've got your back and you can rely on me when the time comes."

Dillon shook his head. "But could you kill a man without hesitation when the time comes?"

Klasson looked troubled. "I'll only know when I'm confronted with possibility, Jake. I've killed no one."

"The first is the toughest, it gets easier after that," Dillon pulled back onto the road and continued driving now and then he gave Klasson a sideward glance, he'd dozed off with his head resting on the side window.

Klasson woke with a start as Dillon hit a pothole and the Citroen flinched a little.

"That business with Finnegan, I want you to understand that I'm easy with that. After all someone would've done it in time. But the violence you dished out, that's what shocked and disturbed me," Klasson blurted out the words.

"Finnegan was a murderer and a scumbag. What he got was what he deserved. If you've no stomach for this line of work. I'd suggest you leave, because my brief is to uncover those involved and drop every one of them at Saint Joachim. Remember what happened to Bergfalk, how Finnegan and Stark sent the Tide Runner to the bottom of the English Channel, with us on it. Stark will not hesitate to kill us if he gets the opportunity."

Klasson remained silent staring out of the windscreen his mind mulling over what he'd just heard and a moment later said. "Why can't we arrest them and let the justice system do the rest?"

"You expect me to answer that ridiculous question?"

"Yeah, I do."

"Well let's start with how we got involved with this assignment. Oh yes, we used false identities, used government money to buy our passage with this crowd, that is most likely going to lead us nowhere. That's entrapment! Then there's the small problem of this bloke Montanari. He could be the man at the top but I doubt it. He's wealthy beyond belief and so well connected that he takes morning coffee with President of the United States. You see where I'm going with this, don't you? The only court that Stark will stand before is my Glock 20 pressed against his temple. Satisfied with that answer?"

Klasson shook his head, "You know in Sweden we have our fair share of serious criminals and I've tracked my fair share of them. I've met villains of all types, but you, you're in a class of your own."

"Which is why I've survived so long in this shitty game," Dillon said. "Now are you in or out?"

"You can count on me. I won't let you down when the

time comes."

"Good, we're about an hour away from this place Saint Joachim, so get more shuteye if you can. I reckon we will need our wits about us. If I was Stark, I would have spotters out in the town for any strangers arriving."

"What is the terrain?"

"Saint Joachim is within the Briere Regional Natural Park, about fifty-four thousand hectares of lagoons and waterways, marshes and in the summer, hot sun. This is the best time of the year, not too many tourists, only a handful of Twitchers in the area."

"Twitchers, what are these Twitchers?"

"Bird watchers, they watch birds." Dillon said.

"So, what in the hell are Stark and the others doing in a place like that?" Klasson demanded.

"That's what we will find out," Dillon said as he slowed the Citroen for a tight bend.

* * *

Olivier Rousseau was forty-five years old, married with two sons. French by birth, he had always lived in Paris. Once he'd graduated university with a degree in Engineering, he applied to join the Foreign Legion at twenty-six. While a serving officer in the Legion he also worked for military intelligence where he worked as part of a team calculating the risk of future Cyber terrorist attacks. On resigning his commission, he worked for the General Directorate for Internal Security and has been there since its start in 2008. This agency encompasses counter-espionage, counter-terrorism and eradication of any potential threats on French territory.

Rousseau has had an adventurous career. Operational on several major terrorist incidents on French soil and around the world and Dillon had had the pleasure with working with him on two occasions.

He was standing beside a Jeep Grand Cherokee, leaning back against the driver's door when they pulled up outside the church. A tall elegant looking man with cropped flaxen hair who looked much younger than his forty-five years.

He walked towards them and greeted Dillon with enthusiasm. "Jake Dillon, my friend, how wonderful to see you again. And I might add, looking so healthy." The Frenchman beamed, Dillon smiled.

"You too, Olivier," Dillon said shaking his hand. "And Corinne and the boys, all well I hope?"

"They are, all of them. She still misses Algiers but we could never go back. I wouldn't last a week if I returned after the last time."

Dillon introduced him to Klasson, and they all got into the Jeep and drove away. It was dark, cold and stormy with heavy grey clouds rumbling overhead.

"What have you arranged?" Dillon asked.

"I gave the whole thing a great deal of thought after Sir Hector Blackwood called me," Rousseau said. "At two a.m. I had a thought, you might say an epiphany, though I say this with all due modesty. To get into the Briere Natural Park presents no problem. To stay without being observed is impossible."

"What, ninety-nine thousand acres of park and a core of lagoon and marsh wetland of seventeen thousand acres and we won't be able to hide?" Dillon said. "I don't follow."

"Oh, the area is vast, but the population is small enough, wild flowers and birds, ecologists and ornithologists. It is the sparseness of the population that makes it difficult for outsiders to enter without being known. What you need is a legitimate reason for being there, a reason which anyone who sees you will accept."

"And you've found it?"

"Yes, birdwatching."

Erik Klasson laughed out loud. "He can't be serious."

"But I am, serious." Rousseau looked offended. "It's obvious, these people come here in their droves just to watch birds and the locals think nothing of it."

"So simple, as you say Olivier. It might work." Dillon said.

"More than that, Jake, I've got the gear to go with it. A small cabin-cruiser and all the photographic kit I could think to bring with me. There's also an inflatable dinghy, waders, camouflaged jackets and night-vison scopes."

"Olivier, looks like you've got all bases covered." Dillon said.

"It's a pleasure, Jake. When my section head told me that Jake Dillon was working an assignment on French soil. I jumped at the chance to come down from Paris to find out what all fuss is. I also have the okay to work with you should you wish."

"Do you want to work with us?"

"I've vacationed in this area since a child and knew it like the back of my hand. You don't, so it would seem sensible." He smiled. "And you do not understand how boring life is these days. A little action would will uplift my soul."

"That's settled then." Dillon turned to Klasson, who was sitting in the rear of the Jeep. "There's nothing like being organised."

"I'm impressed," Klasson said. "I'd be even more so if someone could remember that I need to eat breakfast within the next hour. My stomach has shrunk so much it's hurting."

"That has taken care of, Erik," Rousseau said. "A friend's café is a stone's throw from the lagoon quay. There he and his wife created the most exquisite croissants and make the most delightful preserves. If you are still hungry after this, he makes the most sublime omelette and if you indulge him, you will make a friend for life."

"Take me to this place, that's all I ask." Klasson said.

Rousseau swung the Jeep from one line of traffic to the next, missing a tractor and turned down to the quay.

* * *

The breakfast was everything Rousseau had promised; after eating, they drove down to the old quay, parked the Jeep and walked along a stone jetty. There were flat bottom boats and small cabin day boats of all shapes and sizes tied up to swinging mooring buoys and scores of dinghies tied close to the jetty. They moved down the shallow steps and Rousseau hauled in a six-man inflatable.

Dillon did the rowing and under orders, threaded his way between the boats until they fetched up alongside a twenty-foot fibreglass cabin-cruiser powered by an outboard motor. The boat went under the name of Audrey, white paintwork with polished stainless-steel trim. Klasson climbed, turned and gave Rousseau a hand up on to the deck. Dillon followed, after tying up the inflatable.

The cabin was small, like a tiny caravan, with a bench on both sides and a narrow table in the middle that all turned into a bed at night. The only other amenities were a toilet and a tiny galley area.

Rousseau sat down with a sigh, produced a French cigarette and lit it. Dillon and Klasson sat down on the opposite bench facing him.

"And now, let's get down to business gentlemen." Rousseau said. "You'll find a map in that locker. There's a false bottom, concealing two hecklers & Koch machine pistols with extra clips, and grenades. It seemed like a good idea to bring them."

The map unfolded to show the Natural Park; not only the canals but every lagoon, every sandbank, every waterway.

"You can't go too much by this," Rousseau said. "The tide and the current from the sea combine to create a sandbank one day and then it's gone the next and the waterways can be as precarious. We shouldn't have too much trouble though. Audrey here has a trim bottom; she can stay afloat in three feet of water with no problems."

"And Hades Keep? Have you pin-pointed its location?" Klasson asked.

"But, you won't see it on this map. Let me show you on my iPad." Rousseau brought up a satellite image of a chateau on the lagoon. "Hades Keep, there two miles to the northeast of here." He said pointing at the point on the screen.

Dillon was looking at a small island in a lagoon with a crescent shaped beach on its west shore and sheer cliffs to the east. A grandiose looking chateau lording over the cliffs looked foreboding; round turrets were evident from the satellite image as were the courtyards and grounds.

"Have you found out anything about the layout of the place or Montanari?"

"A little, I've discovered that the chateau is eighteenth century and there doesn't appear to be any detailed plans of the building that have survived. But what I can tell you and as you'd expect nothing links the island to the rest of the park. I spoke to a local woman who used to work at the chateau. She informed me she heard a rumour that a tunnel runs all the way from the cellars to the other side of the lagoon.

Montanari purchased the island from a Russian arms dealer named Nikolay Petrov who was paranoid about privacy; he used to arrive in two helicopters, he would be in one with his personal assistant and bodyguard and the second would have his armed bodyguards in. They'd stay two nights and then leave the same way. Our intelligence report states he is not that concerned to whom he sells weapons.

We have determined his clients are criminal gangs and drug cartels around the world. But before he disappeared he'd been talking in a hotel lobby to a known Chinese cartel member in Europe. This man is now dead. Bullet to the head in a side street in the old quarter of Paris by a suspected contract shooter after he had left the hotel. Nobody has seen or heard from the Russian for over nine months - about the same time Montanari purchased Hades Keep. This might just be a coincidence."

"Coincidence or not, does anyone have any idea what happened to Petrov?" Klasson asked.

"Petrov has been on our watch list for a year now. But, since he disappeared there have been no sightings of him and our analysts have heard no chatter or email traffic from him."

"Olivier, is Montanari in residence on the island at the moment?" Dillon interjected.

"My intelligence is that he's supposed to be arriving later this evening."

Dillon nodded, "All right, I'd better fill you in on the details." His mobile phone buzzed in his pocket. He retrieved it and glanced at the message, placed it back from where it came and carried on talking.

When he'd finished, Rousseau looked thoughtful. Dillon added, "It's been a strange business from the start. Elliott Stark, for example, is he the amateur opportunist making money from wanted and desperate people? Or, a ruthless cold, blooded killer without the slightest scruples, involved with the Macau crime syndicate transporting their people over to England."

"And what of this Feng, does he work for the syndicate?"

"Oh yes, Feng is a syndicate enforcer and a nasty piece of work. But I'm not sure why the Macau crime syndicate sent him or why he is with people like that?" Klasson answered.

"That's what we've got to find out," Dillon said. "Although I've got my own ideas, the Chinese are genius at organisation. But they understand, as we do, sometimes there's a need to keep a safe distance from the where the most liability is. Which is why they're willing to use a man like Stark, amateur or no amateur - mind you, that still doesn't explain how someone like Montanari fits?"

Rousseau nodded. "And what happens afterwards?"

Klasson answered before Dillon could speak. "Dillon's orders are to drop everyone involved."

"Except for Camille De Rosa, she is Italian Interpol." Dillon spoke but his gaze never left Erik Klasson.

"That is if they haven't already murdered her," Klasson said.

The blow came quick and hit the spot. Klasson keeled over and remained unconscious.

"What is this Jake? Is there something I should know?" Rousseau said, alarmed by Dillon's sudden aggression.

"Mr Klasson is not what he seems. The message I received was from Sir Hector informing me that Erik Klasson is dead. Washed up on a beach near Weymouth on the Dorset coast with his throat cut. The attending medical examiner found that he'd had his throat cut by a thin wire. Stark uses a garrotte he pulls out of that fancy watch he wears."

"So, who is this man?"

"Could be that he's one of Starks men. Or, he is Alex Bergfalk who switched identities with Klasson. I don't care who he is," Dillon said, as he used nylon cable ties to bind his hands behind his back and his ankles together.

"What are we going to do with him?" Rousseau's asked.

"Don't worry Olivier; I will do nothing rash to him, not yet. I want to ask him a few questions when he's conscious. Now let's get going, we can get a hell of a lot done before nightfall."

Rousseau nodded. "I'll take us away from the lagoon and into one waterway that will take us away from the hazards along the way. With this engine, we should make it in a little over six hours, allowing for the weather, which I must admit doesn't look too good."

He walked out on deck, Dillon followed him, taking up a position so he had a view of what was ahead. He could also see the inside of the cabin. As the little boat moved off the lagoon, the sky darkened and became ominous as they cut a small wake behind them, rain spotted the deck in heavy drops.

* * *

On the satellite image, the Briere Regional Natural Park covers a vast area of wet marsh-land. All linked by a labyrinth of canals and tributaries that converge and branch off into a maze of smaller waterways.

As they moved in, great banks of reeds and marsh grass lifted out of the water. The heavy pungent smell of the marshes, compounded of salt and rotting vegetation mixed in with the black gaseous mud assaulted their nostrils. This odour that hinted of a darker more primeval world that time had bypassed.

The thunderstorms had not developed as the weather forecasters had predicted and the rain had held off except for the odd light shower. Rousseau kept the small cabin-cruiser safe by steering a passage along the deeper channels towards their destination. Dillon went below to check on Klasson.

"Wake up!" Dillon jabbed the unconscious man with the toe of his boot.

Klasson stirred, groaning as his eyes opened. The dull ache he felt was from the punch to his chin that Dillon had delivered with severity. He opened his eyes, coming back from the knock-out punch he'd received.

"What the fuck, Dillon."

"What is your name and for who do you work?" Dillon's tone was cold. "Two questions - two answers!"

"My name is Erik Klasson, I work for Swedish Intelligence." The words came from between bloodied teeth.

The Glock appeared in Dillon's left hand, the tip of the barrel hovering just above the restrained man's right eye.

"Let me tell you how close you are too dying. I've taken the safety catch off and there's one round already in the chamber. The trigger on this weapon is feather light and only responds to a specific fingerprint, my fingerprint. This gun was built to my personal specification, a subtle squeeze is all it takes."

"I don't comprehend what you're fucking saying. I am Erik Klasson, now untie me."

Dillon pressed the barrel against the eye. "I sent Sir Hector a scan of your fingerprint just before we set off on this assignment, taken from a glass at my house in Sandbanks. That fingerprint caused some head scratching because it doesn't exist on any database, anywhere?" Dillon lifted the barrel of the Glock and stood.

"Look, my name is Erik Klasson and I work for Swedish Intelligence, or that's what my personnel file states and I'm not a field investigator; I work for counter terrorism."

"Prove it." Dillon demanded.

"Untie me."

"Do I look stupid?"

"No, but the proof of my identity is under the skin of my right arm." Klasson said.

After a moment, Dillon cut the cable tie securing Klasson's wrist behind his back and then did the same to the other around his ankles. He kept the Glock trained on the other man as he stood.

Klasson held his right arm out in front of him, "An RFID transponder chip implanted in my forearm. Your smartphone is the standard MI5 issue, I believe?"

Dillon nodded.

"The handset has a military grade RFID reader built in that decrypts the coded information on the chip. If you run it over my forearm, it will detect the information and will come up on the touch screen."

As he held the Glock in his left-hand Dillon held the smart phone over Klasson's forearm with the other. A moment later the information appeared.

Klasson Erik
7,839,025,600,666
Swedish Military Intelligence and Security Service
Counter Terrorism Division

"Okay, so the chip confirms who you are but anyone could have created this information?"

"The thirteen digits will get you conclusive proof. Email the scan to Sir Hector and you'll get your answer."

Dillon looked at the other man, pressed send and waited. He kept the Glock trained at Klasson, sat down on one of the bench seats and waited in silence. Klasson sat down but thought better of it as Dillon lifted the barrel of the 9mm weapon.

The answer came back five minutes later. "Okay, you are Mr Erik Klasson. Your department head has confirmed it's you." Dillon holstered his gun adding, "You still on board Klasson?"

"It takes more than a punch in the face and being hog-tied to scare me. I'm still on board."

"What happens now, Jake?" Rousseau asked. "Do we stop at the village and check in with the park warden or keep going until we reach Hades Keep?

"My instinct says we should stop and check in, perhaps pick up something to eat and drink. Or, we run the probable risk of attracting unwelcome attention from the authorities and anyone else."

"Yes, you're right. We'll tie up alongside that jetty over there and I'll go report in with the warden. You and Klasson go shopping at the stores but beware, Stark will have eyes out reporting anyone new or suspicious back to him."

"We'll blend in then," Dillon's words came laden with sarcasm.

Rousseau ignored him as he manoeuvred the cabin-cruiser alongside the primitive wooden jetty standing out of the water. A hotchpotch of small boats were tied up to moorings, most likely belonging to the occupants of the couple of dozen houses that made up the back-water village. Dillon tied up while Klasson remained inside the cabin.

The Frenchman walked off towards a group of timber-built buildings in search of the park warden. Dillon lounged in the stern, fiddling with the camera equipment that Rousseau had brought with him. There didn't seem to be a great deal of activity on shore except for a man working on the deck of a flat bottom boat. The only other activity was two rough looking men, legs dangling over the adjacent jetty mending fishing nets.

Rousseau returned twenty minutes later carrying a wooden box loaded with various provisions. "Typical French provincials," he commented, as Dillon helped him come on board. "Suspicious of all strangers but they want to know every detail about your business."

"And what did you tell them, Olivier?"

"That I was from Paris with two friends to do a spot of birdwatching and exploring of the park. As I told you before, they get people like that in here all the time."

"And they bought your story?"

"The old woman and her middle-aged son were most helpful when I asked for their help. Once you get them talking, they keep talking." Rousseau laughed. "I asked her where there was a good spot to tie up for the night. This gave me the opportunity to get my map out and point around Hades Keep amongst other places."

"What was her reaction?"

"Nothing very exciting. She told me that the lagoon was private and tourists weren't allowed access there. Although, the present owner hasn't been around for a while, he was always pleasant and polite when he came to the village."

"Fair enough," Dillon mused. "Now let's get away from here and move on towards Hades Keep."

Thunder rumbled in the sky a mile away, Rousseau started the outboard motor as Dillon cast off the lines. Klasson remained inside the cabin until they were well clear of the village, moving along a narrow channel, reeds pressing in on either side of them.

Dillon sat up on the roof of the cabin with a military GPS handset. At first it appeared straightforward to plot a course, but it soon struck Dillon that the deeper they ventured into the marshes, the weaker the signal was becoming.

They had avoided the principal canals and waterways that gave direct access to Hades Keep. They kept to the southeast so were approaching it from the side door.

They'd travelled along the backwaters since early morning, it was now almost dark as they sailed into a small lagoon. Dillon called, "Okay, we'll make this do for the night."

Rousseau cut the motor and Klasson heaved the anchor over the side into nine feet of water. And then it was quiet, except for the natural sounds of the park wildlife.

"How far to Hades Keep?" Klasson asked.

"Quarter of a mile, no more," Dillon answered. "We'll cover the distance in the dinghy just before dawn and look at the place."

"An interesting prospect," Rousseau commented.

"Oh, it should be that, all right."

Above them thunder cracked the sky wide open. As darkness closed in, rain fell in a sudden drenching downpour that sent them all diving for cover inside the small cabin.

HADES KEEP

Chapter 14

> Briere Natural Park
> Brittany
> France

At four-thirty the following morning Dillon stepped out into an unfriendly grey world. Rain hammered into the waters of the marsh with the sound of a hail of bullets falling from a tumultuous sky. The water smudged with each droplet as it ended its journey and yet life still stirred out in the gloom. Birds called and wild geese lifted into the rain.

He wore a full winter wetsuit under a long parka overcoat and a black military stab-proof vest. Dillon fastened a military utility belt holding high-explosive blast grenades, extra clips for both the Armatix and Glock handguns around his waist. Strapped above his ankle a Fairbairn-Sykes double edged fighting dagger with a seven-inch-long blade. A gift from the team at Hereford when he trained with The Regiment there and a weapon he always carried.

Erik Klasson joined him, wearing the same kit, followed by Rousseau dressed for birdwatching complete with binoculars around his neck. Dillon looked him over for a moment

"How do you do that?"

"Do what?" Rousseau said.

Dillon smiled at the Frenchman standing under the large black umbrella. "Look the part wherever and whatever you are doing..."

"I have style, Jake. Something Klasson being Swedish and you being an Englishman know little about." He laughed, looking up into the brooding sky. "I'd forgotten this was such a dreadful time of day."

"Good for the soul, Olivier." Dillon hauled in the dinghy.

"We shouldn't be long, a couple or three hours at most. I want to check the place out and size up the probable resistance we might meet."

"Make sure you know how to find your way back," Rousseau said. "It's not too easy in this place, these waterways are a labyrinth."

Erik Klasson took the oars and pulled away from the side of the boat. In a few moments Audrey had faded into the murk. Dillon used the old-fashioned method of map and compass to plot a course for Hades Keep. In a straight line through mud banks of reeds and narrow waterways penetrating deeper and deeper into a primeval world.

"This place has stood still in time." Klasson commented. "Nothing has changed."

A sound came from the reeds on their left; they parted and three white goats appeared, stopped at the water's edge and watched them.

"Harmless, keep rowing." Dillon said.

Klasson kept rowing until they neared the large lagoon and the towers of the Château loomed up out of the mist around seventy yards away. Dillon made a quick gesture and Klasson pulled into the shelter of the reeds on their right. There was a patch of high ground beyond where they beached the dinghy and got out. Dillon crouched and focused the binoculars.

As Rousseau had said, the Château looked foreboding in style and designed to repel any raiders. The elevations of smooth mortar made them near impossible to climb without specialist equipment. A high turret stood at each corner, impenetrable from below or above and giving a three-hundred-and-sixty-degree view of the lagoon and surrounding marshland. The helipad was in the central courtyard and protected from prying eyes. Whoever had constructed the Château had known how to protect against their foes and yet there was something false emanating from the building.

Too perfect, looked as if it was a film set version of the real thing. Dillon studied the building that had no way of being accessed from the land side. And only a wooden jetty out onto the lagoon. From an approach point of view, the Château had an enviable strategic position. The lagoon looked like a teardrop, two hundred yards across at the widest point and up to five hundred yards long. The possibility of an approach during daylight hours even under water using scuba gear was non-existent.

He passed the binoculars to Klasson. "What do you think?"

The Scandinavian had a look and shook his head. "I don't see how we can get any closer in daylight without being spotted."

At that moment two men came running around the corner of the lower battlement. They jumped into view when Dillon focused the binoculars. Two Chinese, each clutching a machine pistol. A bloodhound running backwards and forwards, alert as it searched every nook and cranny while lifting its nose to the air for any scent.

"It won't get much of a scent in this rain, that's for sure," Klasson said.

"You might live to regret those words," Dillon watched through the binoculars. "That bloodhound can track a fly farting on a cowpat half a mile away."

A commotion over on the right, a heavy splashing as something thrashed its way through the reeds. At first Dillon thinking it might be a guard with another dog, pulled out the Glock in case. And then a low whimper of pain, a splash followed by a cry for help in Italian.

Dillon and Klasson pushed through the reeds emerging on the other side of the sandbank. A man's head broke the water in the channel beyond, a hand flaying around in the air as he tried to get to shore.

Dillon plunged forward, the water reaching his chest. He grabbed for the outstretched hand as the man disappeared under again. Their fingers met, and he went back, the thick black bottom sludge reluctant to let him go.

Klasson helped, and they laid him in the recovery position on the sandbank. At first glance, they thought he might be dead, but he coughed up water and groaned with exhaustion. A tall man with grey-hair of sixty-five who had a gaunt face and looked malnourished. He wore pyjama bottoms and a short-sleeved vest covered in black mud from the lagoon. After his eyes rolled his eyes he talked gibberish with fear and passed out.

"Where did he come from to get in this state?" Klasson

raised a frail arm. "Ever seen such emaciation as this?"

Dillon examined the multiple needle marks and sighed. "Only on a heroin addict and I'd say this one is far gone."

"I wonder who he is." Klasson mused.

Dillon took off his parka. "Last time I saw him I was in Sir Hector's office, he showed me a photograph. He looked healthier and was wearing hand tailored clothing."

"Renzo Montanari?" Klasson said.

"Yes." Dillon raised the unconscious billionaire, slipped the parka coat around him and lifted him into his arms. "Now let's get out of here before he dies on us."

* * *

On the way through the narrow channels, Dillon sat upfront in the dinghy, Renzo Montanari cradled in his arms. He was in a dreadful state, little doubt of that and moaned, crying out and yet never once did he regain consciousness.

The sound of bloodhounds howling from where they'd come from and the harsh chatter of an outboard motor broke the morning quiet.

Dillon held the compass in his free hand. The Sat-Nav was useless in this warren of channels overgrown with reeds and marshland. He relayed precise instructions to Klasson sitting in the stern, the outboard motor clattering, steering the dinghy through the shallow water. At one point, they struck a dense patch of reeds and Dillon eased Montanari to the floor and jumped over the side to make way.

The water was artic, frigid even with his wetsuit, it seemed sub-zero against his skin. As he fought with the reeds, he discerned the sound of outboard motors and dogs howling as they got closer to them.

A few moments later, they broke from the cover of the tributary channel and drifted into open water and Audrey loomed out of the mist.

"Olivier!" Dillon called as they moved closer, saw that Rousseau was sitting in the stern, the awning shielding him from the rain.

The dinghy bumped against the side of Audrey. Dillon stood up and looked straight into Rousseau's face in the shade. He looked at a dead man's stare. Eyes fixed in death, his beaten face had bare knuckles marks that already showed and the small blue hole above the bridge of his nose.

"Good morning, Mr Dillon, welcome aboard Audrey."

Elliott Stark moved out of the small cabin, smiling charismatically as if very pleased to be meeting him again.

* *   *

Feng stood in the cabin by the door, dressed in black tactical clothing. He held a Heckler & Koch HK416 assault rifle carbine that spit out seven to nine hundred rounds per minute with an effective killing range of three hundred metres. He looked grim and merciless, every inch the professional killer.

"You might wonder how we knew where to find you? No, well let me explain gentlemen. One of my men caught you on a covert security camera as you came in last night," Stark appeared relaxed. "We always check on new arrivals in these parts. Imagine my surprise when the image came in to our control room."

"You took your time getting here," Dillon stood in front of Stark. "Not too efficient, are you?"

"It's this wretched weather, old boy. We got here before you left. So, we waited and I have to admit our time has not been disappointing. The late Rousseau became talkative after Mr Feng worked on him. Oh, yes, I now realise that you know something of our business, Dillon. But, we know who you and Mr Klasson are.

"Well, that's nice for you. What's the story with Montanari?"

"Renzo is a necessary problem - he's done this before, it's unacceptable. I must have a word with the person who has been looking after him."

Stark stepped out of the cabin and spoke into a two-way radio. As he turned, Erik Klasson said, "And who hooked him on the opiate, you?"

"The drugs keep him amenable most of the time," Stark said.

"As a zombie, why don't you kill him?"

"Kill him!" Stark exclaimed. "But who on earth will sign the authorisation for the bank transfers?" Stark demanded in a theatrical and half-humorous manner, as if trying to be rationalise the whole thing. He was everything but rational.

Which explained several things. Montanari moaned in a semi-conscious state, thrashing his arms around before sitting up upright. A dinghy powered by an outboard motor appeared from the mist carrying two Chinese guards and a bloodhound. One the men came aboard Audrey while the other and the hound remained in the dinghy. Feng spoke to him in Chinese, so fast that Dillon didn't catch a word. The man replied in a subdued voice, eyes lowered and Feng hit him hard across the face with the back of his hand.

"Has he got a dose with him?" Stark demanded in Mandarin.

The guard put his machine pistol in the floor and pulled a small aluminium case from his jacket pocket. He opened it, took out a hypodermic and a glass ampoule. Stark filled the hypodermic and nodded to the guard who held Montanari by the shoulders. Stark gave him the injection of heroin.

"That should keep him in check."

Montanari stopped struggling and sunk into a relaxed state, tenseness leaving him and a strange thing happened. His eyes fixed on Feng and he smiled.

"Bastard."

And still smiling, the breath left him in a quiet sigh as his head slipped to one side.

A sudden silence. Stark touched his neck for a pulse but Feng moved first. Pushing Stark out of the way he shook Renzo Montanari. He turned, his eyes angry.

"You've killed him, do you understand? You've fucking killed him. I warned you that the dose he was receiving was too much." He struck out at Stark, sending him backwards into the cabin. "It's one fucking blunder after another with you. You'll have much to answer for when we reach Vladivostok."

For a moment, attention focused on the Englishman. Dillon saw his chance, kicking the Chinese guard behind the knee and sending him staggering onto the deck in agonising pain from a snapped hamstring. Dillon spun round and caught Feng in the kidneys with a heavy blow that sent him off balance. Stark lurched forward, a knife in his outstretched hand. Dillon relieved him of it, held the blade and threw the nine-inch knife at the other guard in the dinghy.

The guard in the dinghy had stood; the small craft rocked

making it difficult to keep his balance. Leaning forward he tried to get a shot at Klasson as the knife struck him in the chest, the momentum driving it deep; he slumped, a look of disbelief on his face as he rolled out of the dinghy into the water without even a sigh.

Dillon dived over the rail, surfaced and swam for the cover of the reeds. He threw a quick glance over his shoulder and saw Klasson struggling with Stark on board the cabin cruiser. Feng appeared and struck the Swedish intelligence officer on the back of his head with the butt of a machine pistol. His attention at once focused toward the reeds. Raising the weapon to his shoulder and firing on automatic, emptying the entire clip in a wide sweeping arc. Dillon slipped the backpack he'd left hidden over his shoulders and moved into deeper cover.

Feng and Stark jumped into the dinghy with the Doberman, casting off from the side of the cabin cruiser. Dillon pushed through the reeds, half swimming - half wading. Another sound gate-crashed the morning quiet, the motor of Audrey as she motored away from them.

* * *

He came to a wider much deeper waterway, so deep that his feet didn't touch the bottom. He dived under the surface and swam across to the sandbank on the other side of the channel. Surfaced and forced his way through the reeds. He paused after a few minutes treading water. The sound of Audrey faded. On a heading for Hades Keep, the outboard motor of the dinghy was still clear in the locality. The Dobermans' bark echoed over the stillness of the early morning.

Dillon swam again, pushing his way through the dense reeds; the outboard motor quietened, and the dog stopped barking. This wasn't good, whichever way you looked at it, because now he didn't have the slightest idea where they were.

His feet touched the bottom, thick slippery mud that made his going arduous, he moved out from the cover of the reeds to reach firm ground. The compass still hung on its lanyard around his neck, enabling him to keep track on the direction he was heading in the labyrinth of waterways.

The heavy backpack holding his weapons would drag him under the surface but could be his saving grace. He concentrated hard to remember the map shown on the Sat-Nav screen before it lost connection. The lagoon and Hades Keep was a quarter of a mile away. He climbed out of the water, keeping low to the ground, still, listening and watching for any sound that shouldn't be there. The rain continued to fall from a sky filled with brooding clouds.

He ran, came to a dead stop and took in the landscape before him. It appeared to be more marshland, much the same as he'd struggled through but this was different, more ominous. Taking a hesitant step forward his concern became validated—quicksand.

Moving back into the water, he half walked half swam along the waterway. Keeping to the bank for cover in case Stark and Feng were still looking for him. He kept going, sinking in the thick mud on the bottom until the water became shallow as he approached a sandy shore. There was the sharp sound of a rifle being fired, followed by the sand exploding in a fountain into the air a foot to his right.

The dinghy drifted out of the mist forty feet away. In a single frozen moment of time he perceived and saw the Doberman in the bow of the inflatable. The Heckler and Koch machine pistol cracked again and Dillon turned to run, the Doberman took to the shallow water.

He didn't have long, a minute at most before it ran at him and ripped him apart. He tugged at the backpack until the straps loosened and he was able to release it. Once on the ground he pulled on tactical combat gloves. Found the slim rectangular stun device and with the Velcro straps attached it to the underside of his wrist and waited.

He knew how to handle big dogs. But for him to succeed, he'd have to keep calm and have luck on his side in the first few seconds as the dog came at him.

The Doberman appeared out of the reeds, spotted Dillon, slowed with head low to the ground and without missing a step, moved in, mouth wide, teeth bared. As it launched itself head-on, Dillon raised his outstretched arm. The dog got the full dose of the chemical spray as it grabbed Dillon's Kevlar gloved hand, teeth biting with immense force. And as fast as it had attacked, its jaw slackened with the effect of the stun spray, the chemical taking hold as Dillon pulled his hand back. He moved out of the way as the heavy animal slumped to the ground.

"Sorry dog!" Dillon could feel only sadness for rendering the handsome animal unconscious but survival was paramount. In five minutes, it'd be back up and walking around with nothing more than a slight headache.

Dillon could hear shouting in the distance. Stark giving orders in Chinese to two guards who had joined the hunt and a moment later he heard their heavy footsteps nearby.

It was time to leave. The two Chinese guards wearing black combat clothing came around the corner their machine pistols held on slings by their side in readiness to fire on sight.

Dillon dived for the cover of a clump of reeds and dropped on his face as hefty footsteps crashed through the mud. A cry of dismay as one guard ran into the quicksand. A shot fired and the other guard took a hit from a stray round out of Feng's assault rifle. When he raised his head, he took his chance and got up and ran, keeping low.

Two more shots that came out of the mist, one of them only missing him as he hit the ground again. He moved away from the reeds on his belly, crawling back into the water. A few moments later he reached another patch of dry land, checked his compass and moved northeast towards Hades Keep.

* * *

He took over an hour to reach the point from where he and Klasson had viewed the chateau earlier that morning. He crouched in the reeds and peered across the lagoon. The mist had thickened and everything became indistinct, ghostlike, more than ever a landscape from a Bram Stoker novel.

On the other side of the island, Audrey was moored alongside the landing stage at the rear of the chateau. If their plan was to succeed, this is where it would come from.

To his right, reeds grew out of the mist into the murky water, providing plenty of cover for a third of the distance. The final approach had to be in open water— no other way.

He still wore the wetsuit that clung to him as a second skin, as he moved round towards the line of reeds and waded into the water, staying low. For the first time since escaping from Stark and Feng, he knew he iced to the core and shivered as the water rose higher. His feet lost touch with the bottom and he swam.

He paused as he approached the edge of the reeds and trod water. Forty yards of open water until he had cover again. He took three deep breaths, sank under the surface of the water and swam through the murk, his blurred vision marred with minimal visibility. When he surfaced for air, he turned on his back and noted that he had covered over half way. Dived under again and swam the rest of the distance.

Another minute and his body grazed the mud of the bottom as he neared the Chateau. He came to the surface and trod water for a moment scanning the immediate surroundings for any of the guards. Two Chinese stood only fifteen feet away from him, smoking cigarettes, talking in Mandarin and both slinging Heckler & Koch G36 assault rifles over their shoulders. He made for the cover of a line of reeds on a narrow shoreline and waited.

Crouched in the rain, getting his breath back, he watched the two guards for a moment, could hear them engrossed discussing Stark and Feng. They were young, strong looking, with little or no field combat experience, clear from their oblivion to everything else around them.

He slinked back into the water, half swam, half pulled himself around to a position behind them. Pulling himself up onto firm ground he extracted a ballistic knife from the black scabbard strapped to his leg.

Dillon favoured this knife. He liked it because it had a detachable blade that would release with one press of a button in the handle. Once released it always found its target with lethal effectiveness at distances of up to fifteen feet.

The soft spongy ground made his footsteps silent as he closed in on the two Chinese guards who still stood with their backs to him.

Dillon had always leant towards short and brutal. The strike came quick and without mercy, both guards being dispatched before either could respond. One hand wrenched the head of the smaller guard back while the other holding the blade cut through taught flesh. There was no butchery, just a severed jugular.

As he dropped to the ground, blood sprayed in a crimson cascade across the face of the second guard who at once faced up to Dillon. He was agile but far too slow raising the muzzle of his assault rifle to fire, horror in his face. In that frozen second between life and death Dillon looked into his eyes filled with hatred and released the blade. It pierced the heart as it travelled through the black field jacket he was wearing. He looked in disbelief at Dillon who in the same moment took hold of the blades hilt, twisting it as he withdrew it.

Unseeing eyes remained open in death, the Heckler dropping on to the soft ground beside him from slackening fingers. His heart no longer beating.

"Amateurs!" Dillon said to himself.

The bloodied bodies lay on the blood-soaked ground. He stepped over them as went through an archway of Laburnum up a shallow flight of flagstone steps to another archway. There was a cut grass pathway laid between clipped topiary bushes and tall Italian Cyprus trees. Dillon scanned the surroundings before moving on—there was no sign of life—nothing, and a strange dread touched him. What if they had left? What if Stark had got out while he could? And then Camille De Santi appeared at the end of the ornate garden. Stark was watching from a high window.

* * *

She looked stunning wearing a camel cashmere coat, slim fitting denim jeans and knee-high leg hugging leather boots. The hood of the coat up, she looked the same and yet not the same, a different person. She walked on, hands thrust deep into the pockets of her coat, face serious. Dillon waited until she was abreast of him, then reached out from the behind a large Cyprus tree and touched her shoulder.

Her face remained expressionless but her eyes widened and she had to stifle a cry when she saw it was Dillon.

"I couldn't believe it when Stark said you were still alive."

"He's still here? You've seen and spoken to him?" Dillon kept his voice to nothing more than just above a whisper.

Camille stooped by an early flowering shrub, just in case she was being watched, making as if she were admiring the plant. He spoke only when her back was towards the Chateau. "They came back in the other boat with Sam Savage, though he isn't Sam Savage anymore, nor is he an American but Swedish, did you know this?"

"Yes, how did you find out?

"I heard Stark talking to Feng the other evening."

"How has it been?"

"Disgusting. This man Stark is up to his neck in something with the Chinese Triads and Russian mafia."

Dillon checked that there were no guards wandering around, took Camille's hand and pulled her towards him. Her lips found his and he could feel the warmth of her body against the wetsuit making him stir as a schoolboy experiencing his first kiss. But, their intense yearning for each other had to wait until the assignment was at an end.

"You'd better get back up to the Chateau or Stark might wonder where you are."

"Okay, but you must be frozen in that wetsuit. Go through the stone archway at the top of this pathway, turn right and keep going to the other end. There's a derelict boat-house on the north shore. Wait there. I'll bring you dry clothes and then you can tell me what the plan will be."

As a ghost she faded, and he stood watching her through the quiet rain, conscious of the stillness, exhaustion overwhelming him. He moved off, keeping low and out of sight of any watchful eyes from the Chateau windows, between the Cyprus trees and topiary to the old boat-house.

The ramshackle timber building reminded him of his childhood. The roof leaked and half the floorboards were missing and he slumped against the wall underneath the gaping window. He used to play in just such a place in what appeared to be a million years ago.

He closed his eyes, tiredness flooding over him and then a board creaked. When he looked up, Stark was standing in the doorway, Camille De Santi a step behind him, hands tied in front of her, Feng holding a gun to her neck.

Her face was impassive, softened by the subdued light inside the boat-house.

Chapter 15

Dillon came back to consciousness as if wired up to the mains. No sleepiness, no slow warming up, within seconds he realised the drug he'd had run its course and he was on his feet, eyes wide, dreams not just forgotten but obliterated. He was drinking in the feedback of his senses. Aside from his own noisy breathing, there was no other sound in the room. The room he now found himself in smelt of years of decay and was so dark he couldn't see anything around him. The only thing he could be one hundred percent sure of was the smell of a rat's urine everywhere.

"Klasson, you in here?" he called.

"Over here." There was a movement in the darkness and Dillon reached out.

"Are you in one piece? What happened after I jumped boat?"

"Feng worked me over, wanted to know who we worked for, thought he'd killed me with one of his blows. Lucky for me Stark ordered him to stop and then I passed out with the pain. He's one nasty bastard that North Korean."

"Yeah, he tried that with me but didn't get very far. As he threw his first punch, I swayed sideward, and I caught him in his ribs with a kick. He squealed as at least two of them cracked." Dillon sneered. "Then one of his stooges jabbed me in the neck with a needle and that was it. To be honest, I'm wondering why they haven't just killed us both."

"Did you message London?"

"No, they're using a signal blocker somewhere in this chateau. Our comms are useless. Sir Hector insisted I had an RFID chip implanted just before I left London so they might track that."

The Scandinavian sighed. "Stark isn't such an idiot, is he?"

"Stark is still an idiot and worse, he's an amateur. If the

dying words of Renzo Montanari are to believed, he's involved with the North Koreans, the question is why?"

"So, what's with the people trafficking we are here to investigate?"

"There are no smuggling or people trafficking, now. Well not what we call it in the conventional sense. I think he was onto the authorities long before we arrived to investigate him. Based on what little I've seen I'd say the communists are using him and his cronies to transport something far more sinister than a few dodgy individuals. When we find out who's involved we will find out why they are here."

Dillon moved through the darkness, hand outstretched against the roughhewn wall, slimy to his touch, finger tips dragged over the surface as he made his way. He touched a panel half way up the wall, running his hands around the edge of the two by two-foot square. Once he'd got a firm hold he pulled, and it came away with a splintering crash and light at once came flooding in to the room. He had exposed a window set deep into the stone.

Dillon peered into the opening, looked at a barred window, the glass long gone. At ground level the view opened onto an Italian garden stretching towards the lagoon. The landing stage where the two launches were up alongside Olivier Rousseau's cabin cruiser, Audrey, was visible.

He turned around to find they weren't in a cellar. But a basement room with nothing more than a large circular stone well in the middle of it. Klasson looked at the grille secured by a large padlock over the opening. Dillon had a sense of foreboding as he strained to see what was in the well.

"Must have been the original well." Klasson's voice conveyed fear and tension.

"I reckon, but it's not used anymore." Dillon looked into the semi-darkness.

"How do you know for sure?"

"Because there's enough explosive packed in this shaft to blow the entire building and the island into oblivion."

"Explosives?" Klasson peered in disbelief. "We have to get out of here!" Panic rising in him.

"There's only two ways out. The first is preferable - through a door. The second way is not so favourable!"

"What do you mean? Oh, I see."

"Yeah, you got it. They will destroy this place when they're done here. Erase the evidence and if we're in here when they detonate then that's another problem solved."

Klasson moved around the room, his hands clawing at the roughhewn walls in search of a possible hidden doorway. The room was at least forty feet long by thirty feet wide, the floor had a slight slope running downhill the further along its length Klasson moved.

"In the fifteenth century, this chateau had hidden tunnels constructed. These run under the building towards land and were used as escape routes."

Dillon ignored the Scandinavian. More interested in finding out what device was being used to detonate the explosives. He leaned over the barred opening, beads of sweat rolling over his face, the flashing red diodes of the illuminated timer shone back at him. The pressure was on, the timer had forty-five minutes to run. The voice inside his head goading him, he had come to the end of the road and that this was it. "Go drown yourself." Dillon said aloud

"What the hell man." Klasson looked maddened.

"Not you, this whole situation. This," he waved his hands at the well in exasperation. "we have forty-four minutes and counting to get out of here."

"Forty-four minutes. Are you fucking joking?" Klasson exclaimed.

Dillon looked up. "Yeah, right!"

Ten minutes later Klasson called out. "I've found it, I've found the door!"

"What?"

"Yes. There is a secret door in this wall over here. I knew there must be, just knew it." Klasson cried.

"So, there must be a release trigger somewhere." Dillon stood. "It won't be obvious but it will be in here somewhere. We're looking for loose stones in the wall. Or, one of these flagstones on the floor will stand proud. So that when it's stepped on it releases the trigger. Or, it might be one of those wall sconces that once held an open flame torch. Pull them and push them."

Dillon walked up the steps to the solid oak door, they were both thrown through on their arrival by the guards. He scanned the entire room, looking for a spot where a release trigger could be found. On the other side of the room, Klasson was running his hands over the floor and up and along the walls looking for the elusive loose stone. Dillon came back down the steps and moved to the well.

"Every thirty seconds this receiver handset is vibrating as it signals the sender unit to confirm it's still live. It vibrates again when the signal is transmitting and receiving. Standard protocol for this explosive device."

Dillon could see that Klasson was sweating, that he was right on the edge. This surprised him, the Scandinavian was a trained and experienced field agent and he expected more guts from him.

"Why are you so bloody calm?" The words came out as near hysteria.

"Because, to panic is of no use to either of us, is it!" Dillon had his arm through the large grille right up to his shoulder. He was resting his torso on the edge of the well, scrabbling around for something he'd seen.

The quiet inside the room gone with a sudden release of air followed by the metallic clunking sound of a mechanical lock being released. A few seconds later the heavy stone door awoke from a hundred years of slumber in one smooth action to show a flight of steps leading into darkness.

"What did you do?" Klasson moved across the room.

"The release mechanism had to be somewhere out of sight but accessible enough for a quick escape. The well is right in the centre of the room. In the direct path of the concealed door. It's only when you stand at the top of the steps you can see that." Dillon pointed out as he walked over to the opening.

* * *

They stood for a moment in the confined space just inside the doorway at the top of the steep flight of steps. Dillon brushed away large dust laden cobwebs from the entrance as he searched for the closing mechanism. Klasson trod on the first step which sunk two inches and started a chain reaction that closed the door. With a hefty clunk the door swung towards them and a moment later they were standing in total darkness.

"Well, that's cool!" Klasson exclaimed.

"Move. We need to find our way out and locate Camille before that bomb goes off." Dillon set his smartphone to torch. Pushed pass the Scandinavian and took each step to the tunnel twenty feet beneath them.

An overwhelming dank, river smelling darkness met them as they reached the underground tunnel. Pressure from the lagoon was oppressive above them. The limestone blocks of the arched roof dripped water from between aged joints no more the four feet above them.

Dillon had to stoop in the semi darkness, one hand against the moss-covered walls to steady himself and peered into the gloom.

The floor was awash with mud showing that the tunnel flooded at high tide. The softness underfoot made the going sluggish and released an odour as stagnant as a pond with an undertone of sewage. Every step they made echoed a ghostly cry ahead and behind of them.

The tunnel was longer than Dillon had thought. They moved as fast as possible, crouched, resembling beaten old men in the cramped space that was only three feet wide. At one stage Klasson lost his footing, slipped and fell face into the brown sludge. Dillon smiled to himself as he heard him cursing in Swedish and wishing he'd worn better waterproof boots with more grip.

Dillon could see that the tunnel was veering to the right up ahead, and that they were walking up a slight incline. The ground under their feet had gone from sludge to be more woodland path walking that slight softness of rotting foliage underfoot.

"Keep up Klasson, we're on the way up and out of here."

Dillon quickened the pace and within a minute the half-moon of brightness at the end of the tunnel had widened to receive them again into the daylight.

At the tunnel entrance they stopped and stared at the opening. Overrun with dense thorny foliage, hindering their exit and taunting them to fight their way out.

"Now what?" Klasson said.

Dillon pushed passed Klasson. "We get out!"

After five minutes battling their way through the blockade, they emerged into bright daylight. Looking around, staying low just in front of the tunnel entrance, Dillon scanned the surroundings. They were on the edge of a small wood on the mainland, fifty yards away from the chateau.

Six men passed by only fifteen feet from where they were hiding amongst the undergrowth. Carrying one long wooden create and another large square crate between them they stomped over the footbridge onto the island. Moved through a gate to a gravel path that led to the jetty the two launches and Audrey.

The men weren't Chinese or even North Korean. Dillon listened to them catching the odd word as they passed them.

"Russians," he whispered to Klasson. "Which makes sense. Remember the incident on Audrey when Feng shouted at Stark? He told him he'd have to answer for much when they reached Vladivostok."

"A Chinese crime syndicate, a North Korea contract killer and now the Russian mafia, what the hell is going on here?"

"Something terrible, I'd say. Both crates had a red Chinese symbol stamped on the side of them." Dillon felt uneasy.

"What do you think is inside them?"

"I'd guess that there could be a rocket launcher in the long create. If I'm right, then the square box will contain the tripod that allows it to rotate."

"You're joking, right?"

Dillon side glanced the Scandinavian without commenting.

The men returned from the launch, A few moments later they reappeared carrying two large suitcases.

"Looks as if somebody is leaving," Klasson commented.

Dillon nodded. "Destination Vladivostok. They've got to get out, now we've been nosing around this place. They've no way of knowing others won't follow."

"I still don't understand why they didn't just kill us both."

"They didn't because, I've had a run-in with the Russian mafia on occasions and believe me, they want to take me back to Moscow. Hell, they might even find you useful too, after they've pulped and squeezed you dry of everything you know."

They shrunk back behind the undergrowth as two Chinese guards came running out the Chateau. They crossed the bridge at a jog, machine pistols held and positioned themselves either side of the bridge.

"What's the plan?" Klasson whispered.

"You move off to the left and make sure those guards see

you but keep your distance from them."

Dillon broke cover and moved to the right staying low, Klasson did the same in the opposite direction. He kept to the edge of the wood until he was at least two hundred yards away from where the guards were standing. Then walked back towards them.

As Klasson drew close the guard closest stepped forward raising the machine pistol, the other came forward. Klasson stopped walking, standing still while the two guards advanced on him shouting in Chinese.

Dillon engaged the first guard, used surprise, breaking his neck with one quick fluid movement. There was no sound except for the sharp sound of the vertebrae snapping - death was instant.

The other guard was still walking towards Klasson shouting in Chinese with his machine pistol raised at the Scandinavian. Dillon wasted no time, staying low as he moved closer.

Turning, the Chinese saw Dillon, raised his weapon and fired. The rounds flew wide except for one that ripped through the wetsuit and grazed Dillon's arm. The noise was deafening as he emptied the clip.

Dillon rolled to the left, came up onto his feet. He pounced like a panther and landed on the guard's right side. Knocked him and enabled Dillon to execute a somersault, land on his feet, drop to one knee and release the ballistic blade.

The blade found its target, piercing the guards throat and slicing through the windpipe. Blood spurted in a long arc from the main artery. The guard fell onto his knees hands clutching at the blade, attempting to pull it from his throat as the life drained out of him.

"Klasson get out of sight. Now! There'll be guards swarming out here any second." Dillon shouted.

The Scandinavian moved for the cover of the woods. Jogging to an abrupt halt after only a few paces as a Chinese guard appeared and pointed the barrel of the machine pistol at his head. Klasson dropped on to his knees and raised his hands above his head.

Five black clad figures converged on Dillon, surrounding him, standing and waiting for Dillon to make the first move. This was no ordinary confrontation, they could have shot him where he stood but instead tormented him with their eyes. This was a fight for his life.

These guards were not the same as the others. They were different in the way they moved, self-assured. This signified to Dillon they were military trained and not going to be a pushover as the others had been.

* * *

From deep within his subconscious came the familiar whisper of his alter ego.

'*You know what you've got to do, Dillon. Let me guide you as I always have done, save your life once again. Now count them as they fall.*'

Dillon rolled his head from side to side, releasing the tension, loosening muscles. He looked at each opponent. The scene now black and white, allowing his mind to expand. Visualising the fight unfolding in slow motion. Every move, every punch and kick, every block and counter block that his opponents made - natural elements he used to attack with and defend himself. And how each of the five guards would meet their end. He took a deep breath, the earthy smell of the marsh filling his nostrils.

"Fifteen seconds," Dillon said aloud and set the timer on his watch. He pressed start.

The sense of coiled tension was everywhere as the guards moved first.

Dillon blocked the first punch, countered it with a sidekick to the ribs, taking out the legs from under the attacker in one fluid movement.

His training had taught him one thing, to think like a tiger. This animal was at the top of the food chain, the strongest and deadliest in the kingdom. It moved in one direction, always forward, towards the prey on the offensive.

'*That's the first one, four to go. Now kick their asses.*'

Composing his hands as if he were gripping imaginary tennis balls he launched himself at another guard moving in on him, digging his fingers into the forearm of the swinging arm. Clawing at tendons and muscle, striking the side of the man's ear with the flattened palm of his other hand, bursting the eardrum. The guard left himself wide open. Dillon stepped back, spun and delivered a heavy snap-kick to the other side of his head, broken neck and the spinal cord severed. Death was instant.

'Number two, Dillon. Keep up the pressure. They're amateurs, each working their own fight. Big mistake.'

Dillon ripped into a face to the left of him with his middle and forefinger, raking along the man's nose and mouth. With his other hand, he struck the throat of the guard to his right side. With measured force he dug his fingers in, grabbing his windpipe, squeezing and pulling outwards. Internal tissue and blood vessels torn. Agonising death.

'See how they bleed, how easy they fall. How they die. Now for the rest of them.'

One guard drew a long-bladed knife from under his garb, whirling and rotating it between his hands. Dillon kept out of his strike range, scanning the ground for a weapon. He then spotted the length of rusty chain on the ground six feet away.

He moved with lightning quickness, backwards, forwards, side to side as the guard thrust and swiped the blade at him. As he rolled forward, he fetched up the length of chain, turned and whirled it above his head.

The guard came at him again, the knife held in his right hand. As he sprang forward the end of the chain caught him across the face, knocking him onto the ground. Dillon snapped it back whirled the chain above his head again and released it. As the guard attempted to stand up, he found the full length of the chain wrapped around his neck and upper body. Dillon spun on his right foot, raised his left leg and with full force slammed into the side of his head. The body slumped back onto the ground.

'See what we can do together.'

A double palm heel blow to both ears of the fourth guard, ripping downwards along the cheeks. Result, excruciating pain. Dillon took a punch to his right cheek snapping his head to the side, blood seeped from the open wound.

Off balance, he stepped under and inside of flaying arms to drive an elbow upward into the man's abdomen, taking his centre; he rolled into a palm heel strike to the groin; and back into a rising elbow to the underside of his chin, which linked into another palm heel onto the bridge of his nose.

There were no wasted blows or kicks; each movement rolled into the next.

His body moved from one direction to another. In rhythm to the opposite lines of each attack striking his aggressors in opposing directions and blocking their blows and kicks.

This forced his attackers to lurch into the next stroke head on allowing Dillon to roll into one another and create a tumbling effect.

To Erik Klasson this appeared to be one simultaneous tornado of movement, of blinding speed, a blur too fast for the eye to follow.

Blood splattered from Dillon's nose and mouth. His eyes closed, and he made a gurgling sound, flaying his arms as he flew backwards onto the ground.

He sprang back up onto his feet.

The blood and pain he was feeling in his face generating and pumping more adrenalin through his body. Dillon swayed blocking and countering the guard's kicks and punches.

Dillon struck out around the upper torso and head. One blow caught the guard off balance a second put him on the ground. He stamped the heel of his foot with immense force into the guard's solar-plexus, twisted his whole body and made sure of finality.

'*Watch your back.*'

The first guard was back on his feet. Dillon reacted by dropping to the ground and kicking the legs out from under him. He countered by performing a forward somersault and coming within striking distance of Dillon.

Dillon came up to meet him and launched a double palm heel strike, imagining both of his palms penetrating through the guard's body. He contacted the underside of the man's ribcage, a bone snapped, tissue tore with the force of the blow.

The guard collapsed, lying on his back, bleeding from the various blows and coughing up blood. Death was inevitable and would come.

* * *

The entire fight had taken nineteen seconds. "Impressive." Emotionally and physically exhausted, Dillon felt drained and yet euphoric at the same time.

Klasson came towards him with the guard just behind, pressing the barrel of the machine pistol to the back of his head.

As he was shoved to his knees on the ground, the Scandinavian's face was the pallor of death itself.

The guard could have shot Dillon but had not killed him. He looked at the five men lying dead or dying on the ground, raising the barrel of his weapon pointing it at Dillon's head. The tension in him was audible, he would pull the trigger.

The harsh voice ordered him in Russian to lower the weapon.

He must have been seven feet tall and built the size of a grizzly bear, standing looking at the men scattered around him.

"Impressive, Mr Dillon. These men were from my personal KGB security detail. They have served in my country's special forces regiment."

"We meet again Colonel Petrov."

Dillon dabbed his lip with the back of his hand. "I've got to hand it to you Colonel. You and your friends are full of surprises. Oh, your men fought like girls, it was embarrassing as it only took nineteen seconds to destroy them." Dillon smiled. "Tell me, what are you doing in France with a North Korean, the Chinese and an Englishman with aspirations of a global takeover, or are you nothing more than terrorists?"

Petrov was wearing a radio earpiece, he spoke and the next second four guards appeared. He looked at Dillon, holding his gaze.

Dillon felt the blow to the back of his head and knew what was coming next - slumping unconscious onto the ground.

* * *

Opening his eyes, Dillon at once felt the pain in his head, a blunt reminder of what had occurred. He felt dizzy, disorientated as he tried to stand; soon discovering that he was sitting in a wooden chair of Gothic proportions. His wrists were restrained with cable ties, palms on the armrests. Every time he attempted to free them the nylon bit into his flesh, blood seeped from the wounds. His feet fastened in the same way at the ankles.

A hessian sack had been pulled over his head. Vision blurred making it difficult to see where he was, and with whom. Dillon braced himself for what he knew what was coming.

The chair rocked on its legs as Dillon received the first blow to his face, blood erupting in his mouth from teeth contacting soft tissue. The next two blows came in succession and delivered with expert precision so as not to make him lose consciousness but cause most pain.

Dillon remained still, head slumped, listening, waiting. And then he felt hands grabbing the sack pulling it off his head.

The room was large with windows to three of the four elevations, light flooded in showing opulent furnishings. Elliott Stark was sitting on the edge of a large antique desk, looking at him.

"You, Mr Dillon are becoming an annoyance."

Dillon looked up with contempt in his eyes.

"You and your friend Klasson keep popping up, don't you? Now we know what you are, which isn't surprising."

"What's happened to the man from North Korea?" Dillon asked. "Doesn't he want to have a go as well?"

"He does but at the moment he's busy packing. Thanks to you and your friend, we will have to leave in something of a hurry."

"For Vladivostok."

Stark smiled. "You and Colonel Petrov are old adversaries from his KGB days. But now he has new paymasters and when they see you Dillon they will be estatic."

"Yes, the Colonel and I have met. It's disappointing to see he's reduced himself to a common terrorist."

Petrov struck Dillon across the face with the back of his gloved hand. "I see you are still an impudent dog."

"And you Petrov, it's good to see you haven't changed. When we get to Vladivostok, I hope they'll have adequate hospitality laid on for me."

"Oh, they will take care of you." Stark produced a packet of cigarettes and offered him one. He placed one of the white sticks between Dillon's swollen lips and lit it with a lighter. Dillon was thinking of how he would get out of his present predicament.

If your hands were free, you'd have ripped his head off by now.

Dillon smiled at Stark.

"A friendly warning. The North Korean will want to ask you a few questions when he returns. If you don't give him what he wants, he will inflict as much pain upon you as he can. Feng is an expert in various torture techniques and gets immense pleasure from this. Don't get smart with him. You saw what he did to your French friend on the boat. He will only ask a question once. If he doesn't believe your answer, he will carve you to the bone. The Frenchman sang as a canary after only seven minutes. Once the flesh on his outer thighs had become sliced bacon. I thought he would last longer. I'm hoping you're made of tougher stuff."

"Olivier was a weak man, never had the stomach for blood and gore," Dillon spoke the words. "He was on the verge of retirement, doing me a favour. There was no need to do that to him."

Stark shrugged. "The world over, thousands of people die every day. Your friend Rousseau was just one more. If his death safeguards our cause, then he lived and died to this purpose."

"Word perfect," Dillon spat out the cigarette butt onto the Persian carpet. "Whoever your paymasters are they did a good job of brainwashing you, Stark."

"You don't understand, your kind never does," Stark said. "Once, I believed as you do Dillon. Until I found an alternative way. What I mean is, shown the true meaning of life."

"So now it's justifiable to go around killing people whenever the fancy takes you?"

"Our cause will change the course of history," Stark walked around the chair. "I know you're here to find out what our cause is and why we're involved. You are under orders to kill anyone who gets in your way but you've failed, Dillon. Failed."

"What's one life more or less, mine or yours? We're expendable. Tell me Stark, what have you done with Camille?"

"Ah, the lovely lady from Interpol. I assure you, she is being looked after in the proper way."

Dillon looked at the Englishman with disdain and riled him. "If I remember, your file states that from a young age you were in psychiatric institutions." Dillon paused. "I'm thinking your penchant for murder started at a young age, most likely starting off with small animals and working your way up the food chain to humans. Which leads me to believe you are no different to any other psychopath. Your narcissistic nature demands you be the centre of attention. Which answers the one question, I've asked myself about you, Stark. That this cause of yours is perfect for you because you can live out your sick desires and kill with impunity."

"I thought so. The fundamental difference between us is only in kind. The lesson to learn is that what we do isn't so important as why we do it.

I serve a cause that will create a new world order. Every man, woman and child will know their place in society. Politicians will no longer be in charge, instead the military will rule as it has been proven governments fail the people they serve.

We will have a set of simple rules that will not confuse or hinder punishment. The bureaucratic and judicial systems will make way for military run courtrooms. For instance, if a man kills another man, he too will lose his life by execution. Not go through a weak and impotent judiciary only to enter a prison system that will do nothing other than teach him or her new criminal skills. It's time to bring back the hangman so the scum doesn't become a financial burden on our society.

Can you say as much? What do you defend, Dillon? Capitalism, the Realm, a society that's decaying from lack of discipline and greed, where ordinary people have become so materialistic that the stench of debt is everywhere. God, to think of the years I spent serving corruption."

"That's a well-rehearsed bit of spiel you have there Stark. Must have taken you a long time to put something so fictional together." Dillon allowed himself an inward smile. "The thing is, even with its faults, I'd choose my world over the one you and your crazy friends want any day. How many people have you and your cronies murdered in the last year? One hundred, one thousand, ten thousand, give or take a few for the sake of the cause."

What's wrong with you Dillon. Don't small talk with this asshole. Get out of this shit otherwise you will die in this chair. Now do something.

Dillon noted the look of anger in Stark's eyes. He was now feeling uneasy as regards their plans for him but knew what he had to do next.

He rolled his eyes back, stiffened his body and shook. Drool came out of the corner of his mouth as he thrashed around in the chair.

"What the hell is going on here?" Petrov demanded as he

moved towards Dillon

"He's having a seizure. Get him on the floor, now." Stark ordered.

Two of Petrov's men ran forward, cutting the restraining cable ties from around his wrists and ankles. Dillon slid out of the chair onto the floor and looked unconscious.

Klasson knelt and checked for a pulse in his neck, at once realised that Dillon was okay and figured out what he was doing.

"He's had a seizure, we need to get medical help or he could die." Klasson looked up at Petrov and Stark who were arguing with each other in Russian.

"There is no medical help. No one gets in here. Now take him and his friend to one of the guest suites and you two guards station yourselves outside the room in the corridor," Stark ordered. Petrov protested but Stark talked to him and the two guards carried Dillon between them, Klasson followed with another guard behind him.

Dillon was working out his next move - the sequence would see the two guard's unconscious within five seconds.

* * *

The eyes blink, Dillon's palm snaps up, and the nose explodes, blood erupting. His leg kicks with the force of a mule and the first guard drops to the ground.

His grip on the other guard's windpipe tightened, causing him to stagger. He struggled, trying without success to get free, before Dillon released him.

Bent forward gasping for breath, a knee came up into the face, fracturing his jaw and sending him onto the stone floor. Dillon followed him, wrapped an arm around his neck and twisted. The snap was audible.

"Six seconds." Dillon checked his watch and raised an eyebrow.

Klasson had stayed well out of the way on the far side of the spacious room, came over to Dillon when it had ended. "Six seconds?"

"The time I take to get the job done. You know, one, one-thousand, two, one thousand."

Klasson looked confused and then he realised, "Oh yes, I understand now."

Dillon collected the weapons from the guards, gave Klasson a Barretta 9mm handgun along with an Uzi mini-sub-machine pistol.

"We need to find Camille," Dillon was at the door, cracked it open and checked for any guards that might be outside in the corridor. "It's okay."

Klasson followed, covering their backs as they moved to the top of the stairs.

They both stopped fleetingly, listening for any one moving. They took the stairs to the bottom, crossed the hallway and moved to the closed door on the other side. Klasson stayed alert in case any guards appeared while Dillon listened for any voices inside the room.

Dillon held up one finger to show how many were on the other side of the door. Klasson knew as did Dillon it was Stark.

The handle turned, Dillon pushed open the door. He and Klasson were standing on either side of the doorway. They didn't have to wait long for a reaction. Stark came straight towards them.

Dillon stepped into view, the muzzle of the Uzi pointing at Stark.

"Back into the room, Stark. And keep your hands above your head where I can see them."

"What a remarkable recovery you've made. I should have seen through that little display you put on up there."

"Where are Feng and Petrov?"

"They're on the island somewhere."

Dillon stepped forward striking Stark across his face with the Barretta. Blood flowed at once from the gash on his cheek.

"I'll ask you again - where are Feng and Petrov?"

"On the jetty making the boat ready to leave."

"That's much better, Stark. Now sit in the chair you had me tied to." Dillon turned to Klasson.

"Watch the door, shoot anyone who tries to enter."

Klasson watched the door while Dillon asked Stark questions.

"The service you've been running for illegal entry into the UK, was this your enterprise?"

"No. It was Finnigan's enterprise, he'd been running illegal immigrants across the Channel by the boatload. He wasn't fussy who they were as long as they could pay for their passage. It was easy to have our people aboard the Tide Runner on odd occasions."

Clever move. Dillon nodded.

"How many of your people are in the UK?"

"If I told you how many, you'd be sick."

He sneered and Dillon put the Barretta to his temple. "Don't get smug or I might just put a bullet through your elbow."

Stark looked up at Dillon. "I lost count after the first five hundred. And, before you ask, yes, these people are in the UK. We have ensured through our network they are working in positions within the Civil Service and the Ministry of Defence. Where they can do the most damage to the ruling government. Finding them will prove impossible."

"Nothing's impossible, Stark."

"Well, let me enlighten you. Each and everyone one of them is the holder of a valid British passport, driver licence and bank account. What you can't see, you can't find. Their files along with many others get regularly checked by the intelligence service. Much better to be there and yet not there if you follow me."

"What of Renzo Montanari. Your cause used him for his wealth and then fed him heroin?"

"I first met Montanari while at a centre in Milan that specialised in drug addiction. I was there to clean up or lose my trust fund. Montanari was addicted to drugs for years. One evening I was sitting in the communal television room when he came in and sat in the chair next to me. He was ill, that much was clear, and thought he would die.

And that was the start of a fruitful friendship. He came to, how shall I put it, depend on me? When I gave up the booze and drugs, I persuaded Montanari that he needed quiet and isolation. So, he bought this place under the name of one of his off-shore companies. He was in decline by then and the primary reason he had become a recluse. I've looked after him for the past four years."

"In between assignments for your paymasters in North Korea and Russia."

"My North Korea paymasters, Dillon, let's get it right. Our friends in Vladivostok have proved excellent allies and a useful gateway to Europe for our cause. The North Korean regime have found me invaluable, for obvious reasons. They're in a tricky position at the moment with their missile testing. One wrong move and it's all history."

"Well, your paymasters will not praise you when they hear of this fiasco, will they?"

"Oh, I don't know. We have our people in position and located where they can rally the masses when the time comes. They will be ready and waiting for the signal to put our strategy to take control into action. Once these sleepers are activated they will carry out their task, even if it means the ultimate sacrifice of death."

There was nothing Dillon could say could erase the faint, superior smile from Stark's face. And then he recalled something he'd read in his file.

"I was forgetting. I have a message for you." He lied with complete conviction. "From your twin brother."

The effect was shattering. Stark appeared to shrink. "Kingsley?"

"That's right. You thought he was dead, didn't you? But we found him and he was forthcoming with information regarding you." It was Dillon who now had the smile on his face.

"How is he?" Stark's voice was a whisper.

"Very alive. He asked me to let you know each day he remembers what you did to him all those years ago. He was particular I should tell you that."

Starks face had turned pale, and he spoke through clenched teeth. "I don't care what he thinks of me. He is dead and forgotten."

"Dillon," Klasson hissed. "There's someone going to come through the door." The Scandinavian dropped to one knee, raising the Uzi up to his shoulder, he took aim.

Dillon sat on a chair opposite Stark with the Barretta levelled at his abdomen.

The door opened and Camille De Santi emerged. She was wearing a raincoat and carried a weekend bag. She glanced at Dillon, holding eye contact with him for the briefest of moments and yet time stopped when he saw her.

A moment later Feng appeared, saw Dillon and Klasson raised his gun and fired. The bullet flew wide, Klasson reacted, his Uzi spitting two rounds into the North Korean's chest.

His body flopped with a wet, fleshy thud onto the ground. Klasson kicked the semi-automatic away from the body, knelt on one knee checking for a pulse.

"He's dead?" Dillon asked.

Klasson nodded, "He deserved to die for what he did to Olivier Rousseau."

Camille De Santi stared at the dead North Korean now lying in a crimson pool of his own blood. Dillon was scrutinising her reactions and her defiance to her captor, Elliott Stark. There was something askew with her and he couldn't put his finger on what it was.

He stood up striking Stark across the face with the open palm of his hand. The sound of the slap was like a whip being cracked. Stark fell onto the floor disorientated rolling over, holding his hands and arms up for protection.

Camille rushed forward to help him and confirmed to Dillon what he had suspected. That she was a good actor, or had feelings for Stark. He held her arm as she helped him to his feet.

"What was that for?" Stark asked wiping blood from the corner of his mouth.

"To confirm a theory, I've had for a while!"

"A theory?" Stark's voice was incredulous.

"A theory."

Dillon walked over to the door, keeping his gun trained on Stark, opened it and told Camille to go the jetty and wait on Rousseau boat.

"Camille, you'd better take this," Dillon handed the Uzi to her. "Petrov and his men are still here."

She took the weapon, her face blank as if he wasn't there and walked out.

As he closed the door Dillon said, "What did you do? Spike her drink?"

Stark swung round with a rancorous look on his face. His hand dipped into his jacket pocket emerging with a small pistol he pointed at Dillon's face.

"If you intend to shoot me, Stark. You'd better be quick or my friend will shoot you." Dillon smiled and then snatched the tiny weapon away from him.

Loud voices came from outside in the hall. It was Petrov

giving orders to his men. Dillon motioned for Klasson to get out of sight. He could visualise the former KGB colonel pushing on the handle from the other side but then changing his mind as the door didn't open at once. When it moved and as he finished talking, he entered the room filling it with his huge presence.

Dillon was sitting in the chair, an Uzi mini sub-machine pistol hidden from sight by his side. Stark stood in front of him with a Barretta in his hand, minus its clip.

"Trouble?" he enquired in Russian.

Klasson had disappeared behind one of the long sofa's out of sight.

"No, Petrov. There is no trouble, Mr Dillon wanted to talk, so I humoured him." Stark was acting the awkward pupil caught out and having to justify himself to the head-teacher.

A look of contempt appeared on Petrov's face. He walked towards Dillon, hands behind his back and when he was close enough punched him in the stomach.

The blow was perfect, the work of someone who knew martial arts. Dillon could appreciate that much before he leaned forward and vomited over the Russian's boots.

"That is for killing my men."

"Reckon I can give you that one, Petrov." Dillon wasn't ready to kill the Russian, just yet.

* * *

He sat in the chair, leaning forward concentrating on recovering his breath while the voices droned somewhere on the far side of the room, indistinct, meaningless. The Colonel's fist had not caught him in high in the stomach, where such a blow could have killed him but in the lower abdomen by design.

Dillon had tensed his muscles to receive the blow. Although sick and sore, he was recovering when the two Russian guards lifted him.

He played it to the hilt, dragging his feet on the way out and groaning. They took him across the hall and descended to the cellars and well room. When they reached the cellar, they dropped him on to the flagstone floor. The one who carried the Uzi over his shoulder now unslung it, holding it ready in his hands while the other got out a key and unlocked the door.

The man with the machine pistol leaned and grabbed Dillon

by his hair, pulling him to his feet. Dillon drove the stiffened fingers of his left hand under the chin into the exposed throat, a killing blow when delivered. The man didn't even choke, sagged to the floor as if he were an old sack, dropping his weapon.

Dillon came to his feet and lifted his elbow into the face of one man. The surprised Russian gave a stifled grunt and stumbled backwards into the well room. A strong hand jerked the man around and Erik Klasson hit him once in the stomach and another in the jaw.

In the silence, Dillon picked up the Uzi and grinned. "How he hell did you get out of that room?"

"When I rolled over the back of that sofa, my intention was to hide there until everyone had left the room and then sneak out to find you. But I landed heavily and slammed against the wall. The panelling flipped inwards taking me with it and dumping me into a hidden passage that led the way to a hidden doorway along the passage back there." Klasson pointed into the darkness.

"Incredible."

"What's our next move?" Klasson asked.

Dillon held up the Uzi. "Even with this, we stand little of a chance against Stark, Petrov and those Russian Spetsnaz soldiers. If we can get on board Audrey, things become different. Rousseau had concealed hand grenades and two Heckler & Koch MP 6 assault rifles with extra clips behind a false panel in the forward bulkhead. That will more than even things."

"What of Camille De Rosa?"

"Not sure. I think she might have been playing us for fools. She's had it."

He cut off any further discussion by leading the way outside and trying the other end of the passage. The first flight of stairs they came to had a door at the top, that was unlocked. When Dillon opened it, he looked into the kitchen, a large square room with a fire burning on an open hearth. At that moment another door opened and two of the Russians entered. Dillon closed the door, put a finger to his lips, and they retreated. At the far end of the darkened passage, more steps took them to a door long disused. Klasson grappled with the rusted bolt until it moved and the door opened. The garden was surrounded by a six-foot brick wall neat gravel paths and maintained borders.

After waiting a moment, they jogged out through an archway at the far end and ran for the shelter of a clump of trees.

Making it, they kept ongoing, Dillon in the lead, following one path towards the jetty.

Without warning, the path ended at a clearing on the edge of the lagoon in which stood a large circular timber sun deck. The roof was something else, curved glass in solid oak frames. Camille De Santi was standing there, staring out across the still water, hands in the pockets of her long cashmere coat.

She swung round, startled, the barrel of the Uzi pointing straight at her with puzzlement appearing on her face. Dillon dropped his machine pistol and grabbed her, clamping a hand across her mouth.

"Listen and you listen good. I don't know what you're up to but you are seconds away from death. Do you understand?"

She gazed at him, wide-eyed and he took his hand away. At once she opened her mouth to cry out and Dillon had no choice but to strike her across the back of the neck with his open hand. The blow rendered her unconscious but unharmed otherwise.

He lowered her to the ground and turned to Klasson. "Sling her over your shoulder and make for the jetty. Get as close as you can and wait in the bushes."

"What are you going to do?"

"Create a diversion. If I can draw them off, it will give you time to board Audrey and get moving."

"What are you going to do?"

"I'll swim out from here and catch you on your way past and don't go getting heroic on me. Just make sure you get out of here."

"You're in charge."

The Scandinavian hauled Camille up and slung her over one shoulder and moved away into the undergrowth. Dillon retrieved the Uzi and hurried back up towards the house. He had a plan of sorts. The chateau had was built out of stone but had a vast number of timbers throughout the building. With the right encouragement it should go up with the gusto of a fifth-of-November bonfire and there was one obvious place to start.

He moved back through the gardens and entered the basement again. Petrov and his men were nowhere to be found. This time, when he opened the door at the top of the second flight of stairs, the kitchen was empty.

He entered, found the hose that delivered the liquid petroleum gas from the underground storage reservoir to the cooking range and yanked it free from its connection. The hissing came with a sudden rush settling as the gas escaped into the room.

Dillon looked around for the electric toaster; moved straight to it and rolled up pages from an old newspaper he'd found inside one cupboard. He wedged them in the toaster slots and pressed to engage the power. The heat in the elements rose, and the paper smoked.

Behind him, the door opened and Colonel Petrov entered.

If he had a gun, it didn't show and the machine-pistol had him covered.

Petrov smiled. "No sporting chance, Mr Dillon?"

"You and your cronies didn't give Olivier Rousseau a chance." Dillon spoke with a menace as he edged his way back to the outside door. He kept one eye on the toaster and the other on the Russian. He only just made it as the paper caught light and a second later the gas ignited.

When the explosion came, it brought with it an intense fireball, blowing out the glass in the windows and the door that Dillon had just come through off its hinges. Everything inside the kitchen including Colonel Petrov became engulfed in the flames within seconds chasing Dillon as he rushed outside to escape.

As he ran out through the garden, the thought of the explosives in the well room below the chateau stayed with him. The explosion would not only destroy the chateau but would take out most of the island.

He stopped for a moment, listening. He could hear cries of alarm from the other side of the chateau. The Russians by the sound of it, running to see what had gone wrong. Just as he had hoped.

He gave it another minute, then ran for the trees and the pathway leading to the edge of the lagoon. Audrey's motor burst into life over to his left. So Klasson had made it? Behind him there was a sudden crackling as flames exploded through the first-floor windows, blowing out the glass.

A bullet splintered the trees above his head. He dropped onto one knee and emptied the clip of the machine pistol in a wild burst. The Russian shooter, although wounded, managed to retreat around the corner of the burning building.

Dillon ran as shots chased him, slicing through bark and foliage on either side of him. He burst from cover and plunged headlong into the lagoon as Audrey appeared round the point sixty yards out.

As he swam, Klasson altered course to bring the cabin cruiser closer to him. As Klasson spun the wheel and cut the motor, the boat slewed to a halt broadside.

The Scandinavian ran for the rail and pulled Dillon with easy strength.

"Get us moving and make it quick," Dillon gasped.

As Klasson vanished into the wheelhouse, a bullet ricocheted from the rail as the first Russian arrived at the water's edge. Dillon turned and saw Elliott Stark appear from the pathway with another three men. The engine roared as Klasson pushed Audrey to the limit in their haste to get away in a burst of speed, bullets chopping into the hull.

Chapter 16

Once around the southern tip of the island they were out of the direct line of fire and safe for the time being. Camille De Rosa lay on the deck in the stern of the boat where Klasson had left her. She was unconscious but when Dillon picked her up she groaned and her eyes briefly opened.

"What did you do?"

"She was trying to get free."

"You whacked her?"

"Oh, god no. She slipped on the jetty and caught her head on the side of the boat as she fell. I had to manhandle her on board and that's where she landed."

Dillon took her into the cabin, gently laying her on a seat, opened the forward locker and pulled out his black military combat clothing. He unzipped and pulled off the wetsuit, threw it on the floor and put on the dry clothing, he removed the false bottom in the locker.

He hooked grenades to the bullet-proof jacket. Filled the outer pockets with extra clips for the two Heckler and Koch machine pistols he was taking and moved out on deck.

Klasson was giving the motor everything it had and Dillon shook his head. "We're wasting our time. That rib they have has three times the speed. We've got maybe five minutes before they are alongside us. So, let's prepare and be ready for them, reduce our speed and let them catch us."

"What do we do?"

"Fight the best way we know how. I'll show you how to use one of these." He gave the Scandinavian one of the machine pistols. "When you fire one of these, don't shoot from hip height as you did. Fetch it up to your shoulder and aim it the same as if you were firing a hunting rifle. That way you're guaranteed to hit wherever you aim. We have little ammunition, so only short bursts."

Dillon gave Klasson four of the grenades. "Remember, you've got four seconds once you've pulled the pin and don't you forget it. We've each got four grenades, carry them in your coat pockets."

He looked back through the mist to where smoke drifted through the heavy rain.

"I shouldn't think there's much of Hades Keep left after that unfortunate gas explosion. Kill the motor, let the boat drift."

Somewhere not too far away, the engines of the rib roared into life. They had entered a much smaller lagoon and Audrey moved broadside towards a narrow waterway at the far end. She drifted to a halt, her prow in the reeds and Dillon nodded.

"This is as good a place as any. Get Camille up on deck and I'll tell you what we do next."

* * *

The still waters of the narrow waterway rippled as the rib moved towards the mouth of the small lagoon. One of the Russians stood in the prow, machine pistol held ready, saw Audrey and cried out.

The outboard motor became quiet as the rib moved on, carried by its own momentum drifting past the place where Erik Klasson stood waist-deep among the reeds. A hand clamped over Camille's mouth, securely holding her.

Dillon waited on the other side of the lagoon on a piece of high ground, soft sand surrounded by marsh grass. Two grenades lay on the ground beside him, another was ready in his hand.

He glimpsed Stark's flaxen hair in the stern and then the rib was abreast. It was eighteen or twenty feet away from him when he tossed the first grenade. It bounced on the side of the inflatable, landed in the water and exploded. The whole rib rocked in the turbulence and there was a cry of alarm from the Russian in the prow as he blown headlong in the water.

On the other side of the lagoon, Klasson pushed Camille De Rosa away from him, took a grenade from his jacket pocket, pulled the pin and tossed it. The rib was further away from him and he had to throw it with more force but it still fell short, sending a fountain skywards. As he took hold of another one, Camille flung herself on him as he threw it. It fell only fifteen feet away and the blast flattened the reed and knocked them back into the water.

Klasson surfaced, reaching for Camille. He found himself under heavy fire from two of the Russians crouched in the prow of the rib, their machine pistols resting on the edge. At the helm Stark gave the engine full power, spinning the wheel as the propeller created a maelstrom around them. In the same instant, Dillon's second grenade exploded just behind them, taking out the fibreglass stern board and outboard motor with it. The rib shuddered and bucked as a raging bull. As it slowed, Dillon tossed his last grenade. It landed where he'd hoped, in the prow and exploded with shattering force.

Stark was at that moment picking up a machine pistol from the deck ready to fire in Dillon's direction when the blast lifted him and bowled him over the side and into the water.

The rib sank from the gouge in the fibreglass hull and the inflatable sections were torn open by flying fragments. The two Russians crouching in the prow continued firing towards Klasson. Dillon moved a few yards to his right, to a place where he could get a good view; drove them both overboard with a short burst from his machine pistol.

There was a fleeting moment when unnatural sound dissolved and the calmness of the marsh returned. Klasson heard the bullets hit the Russians, the dull thud as they found their targets and a moment later the percussion of the weapon used.

And then it had finished as fast as it had started. The only sound was that of Camille De Rosa floundering through the shallows, trying to pull free from Klasson's grip.

Dillon slung his machine pistol and swam towards them. When he was close enough to their side of the lagoon, he waded through the water, reaching for the Camille's free hand. She was thrashing with a strength that surprised both men.

"Drugged, I'd say." Dillon hauled her through the shallow water and up onto a sand bank. He released his grip, and she flopped on to the wet ground, Dillon knelt beside her. The look on her face was frightening, eyes rolling, her mouth was foaming and temperature sky high.

"Klasson get over here. She's having a seizure."

"What the hell did Stark give her? Let's get her on her side in case she's sick."

They rolled her in to the recovery position. Dillon

supported her head in his lap while Klasson held his water bottle to her lips to get her to drink. After two minutes everything changed. Camille sat up as if nothing had happened.

"Where am I, what's happening?"

"It's okay, Camille," Dillon stroked her hair and held her. "You've been drugged by Elliott Stark."

"Drugged. But how and why?"

"Slipped into a drink to keep you compliant. Most likely since you arrived here. Do you remember anything?"

"I only remember thinking I should stay with them to find out where they were going. But after that everything is a blur."

Dillon heard movement out in the water and then it happened as if was something out of an apocalypse movie.

Stark surfaced in shallow water, amongst the floating wreckage that looked something from a film set, his clothes soaked in blood. That strange ascetic face calm, devoid of expression, the wet flaxen hair plastered into his skullcap.

Camille looked at him, pure hatred in her eyes as she reached for Dillon's machine pistol laying on the sand. In the same instant Stark's hand drew right back and there was a flash of steel in flight.

Everything happened at once. Camille, still trying to grasp the machine pistol just out of her reach, floundered across Dillon's path and the knife buried itself in her chest. The black handle protruded from beneath her breasts, blood oozing from the narrow wound.

Stark came out of the water with a cry of anger, lurching towards where Dillon was supporting Camille as she staggered. Klasson emptied the machine pistol into him, driving backwards into the water, he disappeared under the surface and the current took him with it.

Dillon caught Camille as her legs buckled, a look of complete surprise on her face. He held her tenderly and in the same moment the life drained out of her. She hung for a moment in his arms and then he lifted her. Klasson was standing in front of him and cried, "Is this what we came for, this butchery?"

He threw the machine pistol into the water, turned and waded through the shallows to where Audrey up against the reeds. Dillon followed him and as he scrambled over the rail, Klasson took Camille's body and between them they laid her on the deck.

The boat moved, pushing its way through the narrow waterway, emerging a few moments later into the main channel. Beyond, through the rain the smoke drifted up from Hades Keep. Dillon knelt by the rail, glancing now and then at Camille. The bitter weather was unbearable, causing him to shiver, draining him of feeling.

And then he realised a strange thing, he was still clutching Stark's knife in his left hand. The channel widened as they moved through the estuary out to sea and he stared at the black throwing knife he'd pulled from Camille's chest.

"And how many dupes have you dispatched in your career, Dillon?"

The words came as a whisper in his ear as if Stark himself had spoken. In a sudden gesture of revulsion, Dillon flung the knife over the side, it glinted once as the light caught the blade, then sank beneath a wave. Somewhere overheard gulls called as they moved out to sea and he rose to his feet to join Erik Klasson in the cabin.

Epilogue

Early morning sunlight flooded through the tall skinny window of the study. Dillon gazed at the rays travelling over the back wall while he waited for the video link to be secured with London, knowing he was being watched.

Bright bulbous eyes scrutinised his every move. Both French Bulldogs sat on their haunches ogling Dillon with wide eyes. Their attention turning to the wall screen as a face appeared. From behind horn rim specs, Sir Hector Blackwood spoke to Dillon.

"Congratulations on a job well done, Dillon. The conspiracy you exposed in France has had every section head ordering a security lockdown in Whitehall. The Prime Minister is convening a COBRA committee this afternoon."

Cabinet Office Briefing Room A (COBRA) is part of a group of meeting rooms in the Cabinet Office at 70 Whitehall. In most cases Cobra is convened as part of the civil contingencies committee, which plans government responses in times of emergency.

"The Director General of MI5 briefed the Prime Minister last evening who ordered the immediate inspection of all personnel files across all departments. One hundred and forty-seven suspects were uncovered using the latest risk assessment algorithm. One thing linked all these individuals."

"And that was?"

"Every one of these people had the same heavily encrypted web browser loaded on their desktop computers and phones. The only reason anyone would have this is for viewing content on the dark web."

"Right up to the end, Stark remained self-assured we'd never find the sleeper agents placed within our civil service, well he got that wrong."

"The Cyber Investigation department discovered a heavily encrypted page on the dark web linked to a number of terrorist groups in Europe. This was regularly visited by each sleeper. These men and women have now been arrested under the prevention of terrorism act and are being detained at an undisclosed secure location for assessment and processing."

"Have we discovered who gives the orders. Is it the North Koreans, the Russians or the Chinese?"

"Yes and no. It's proving almost impossible as these people are nothing more than ghosts, protected from the law with diplomatic immunity or armies of lawyers. As for digitally tracking them, they are protected behind advanced Chameleon cloaking software that creates havoc with our systems."

"So, what happens now?

"The cyber unit searches for the trail that leads to those involved at the top of this conspiracy. As for you, Dillon, take a holiday. I'll be in touch when I have something for you."

The connection terminated.

Dillon looked at the two French Bulldogs sitting on the sofa.

"Guys, it looks as if we're flying to Scotland.

Until the next time...

THE END

Printed in Great Britain
by Amazon